MURDER
IN THE
MONASHEE
MOUNTAINS

A Travis Daniels Investigation

JP BEHRENS

Crystal Lake Publishing
Where Stories Come Alive!

www.crystallakepub.com

WELCOME
TO ANOTHER

CRYSTAL LAKE PUBLISHING
CREATION

Join today at www.crystallakepub.com & www.patreon.com/CLP

*For James A. Moore.
You are missed.*

*And for Stephanie.
Love Always.*

Contents

Lanford, Illinois

I burst through the door of our rented cottage, made for my bedroom, and started jamming clothes into a suitcase.

"We need to get out of town by nightfall," I called out to Leslie, who was poring over three ancient tomes.

"What?" Leslie's bare feet slapped like the rapid-fire applause at a Buster Keaton film as she raced to my door. "What are you talking about? We've finally settled in."

"Doesn't matter. I made a Fed wandering around town asking questions. Found more milling about in front of the grocer's and farm stands. Likely, they caught wind of the moonshiners in the woods sending hooch into Chicago." I slammed the suitcase closed. "I don't plan on being here when they raid the place."

"Are you sure they were Feds and not random strangers victimized by your constant paranoia?"

"I'm not that paranoid, and we're not sticking around long enough to see if I'm right or not. Now get your stuff together and in the car."

Leslie stomped after me. "I'm sick of running, Travis. I was finally getting comfortable with the neighbors, with going out and talking to people again. You even managed to establish a credit line with the grocery store. Just because you've lived your life broken off from other people, relying on your own, doesn't mean I want to."

I paused long enough to meet Leslie's distraught eyes. Though she'd been through so much, Leslie remained a young woman who should have been finding herself and building a life, not running from one small town to the next as a fugitive. "I get it, Leslie, but with Capone an hour north of us and the FBI lurking around every corner searching for the bootleggers supplying him, we can't be here when the press arrives. One picture of us in the background while the authorities are hauling half-drunk, backwoods brewers to jail will be the end for us. The story and pictures will find their way to all the papers in New York. We need to go."

"And if I refuse?" Leslie planted her fists on her hips and stood in the center of the living room, daring me to force her.

I sighed. "Then Mandeville will discover you're alive, hunt you down, and sacrifice you to whatever dark god he thinks will give him more power. You know that." And she knew how much I hated repeating it. "After everything that happened in Arkham, I have no intention of tempting fate."

Muscles on both sides of Leslie's face rippled with fury. I returned to my room to gather more clothes, throwing them into the nearest empty bag available. Wrinkles, neatness, and order were no longer a concern. She stomped through the house. I heard books slapping closed and angry mumbles as she packed her belongings. Good. She wasn't happy about it, but she understood we didn't have any other choice.

"Do you remember that spell I told you about?" Leslie asked from the other room.

"The invisibility one?"

"If I can get the ingredients, I think I can hide us."

"I don't like all this magic stuff. Everything I've seen so far is dark and twisted. I'd rather not rely on any of it."

"I know you don't want to deal with the same dark powers my uncle does, but we are leaving available resources unused in this fight. I just want to put a little of it to work defending ourselves."

I came out of my room with a second bag bulging with clothes and personal hygiene necessities. Leslie had the pouch she'd enchanted to hold an endless number of objects hanging from her shoulder.

"Go pack your clothes," I instructed.

She rolled her eyes and pushed past me toward her room.

The door slammed closed behind her. She wasn't going to be very fun once we were on the road.

Outside the cottage we'd been renting, I scanned the street for any unwelcome eyes. It had been almost a year since Arkham. During that time, Leslie and I lived on the move. The seclusion of this farm town surrounded by thick forests should have been enough to stay off everyone's radar. But groups of bootleggers, who shared similar notions, set up camp within the forest while living in the small community. It was only a matter of time before someone with a deep love of Prohibition or a badge noticed the growing population of glossy-eyed, mindless stiffs stumbling and moaning through town at night.

It took us less than an hour to pack our meager belongings, drop the keys and last month's rent in the mailbox, and set out. The money Mandeville had paid me for the task of finding Leslie was running out. I'd picked up different day labor jobs where I could, but work was getting more and more scarce in the Midwest. I needed to start getting creative to earn money.

"What do you need for this spell of yours?"

"I've gathered most of what I need, but I'm missing one ingredient, a rare flower."

"And then what? We become walking ghosts or something?"

"No, but if I'm right, we could walk into a bank vault during business hours, take two sacks of money a piece, and no one would bat an eye as long as we don't break out into song and dance mid-heist."

"We are not robbing a bank." Not yet, at least.

"I didn't suggest we should. I was just illustrating the potential of the spell."

"How sure are you this spell will keep us hidden from magical detection?"

"Pretty sure?" Leslie shrugged. "My books don't really go into how effective the spells are, only what they do and how to cast them. From what I translated, as long as we don't do anything that demands notice, everyone's attention will slip over us as if we are invisible."

"I guess getting coffee at a diner would be out of the question."

"No, as long as you wave down a waitress, say hello, or cough, someone can see you until they look away. How much they want to remember you or you want them to remember matters somehow. The minute you leave, however, all memory of you will vanish unless you make a really big impression, or the person focuses really hard to overcome the spell."

"Big impression?"

"Like pulling out your gun and robbing the place. That would keep you in their memory for a while. But not indefinitely."

"Good to know."

Leslie dug out a map of the country. I was adamant we stayed clear of any major cities. Mandeville seemed like the kind of man who was well connected, and I refused to risk our safety for the smell of concrete and civilization. Leslie didn't mind the wide-open sky as much as I did. She was a country kid from birth. I was the hopeless city rube out in the open pastures of America.

Using a small crystal on the end of a string, Leslie spoke impossible words over the map. The crystal pulled to the left.

"What are you doing?"

"Looking for the last ingredient."

"I didn't agree to do the spell. I was only making conversation."

"I never asked for your permission, and I don't need it. If you don't want to try the spell, fine, but I want my life back. If this is the first step toward that goal, I'm willing to risk it."

"What if Mandeville feels your power or something?" I was grasping at the illusion of leverage to get her to slow down and think.

She smiled. "The spell isn't powerful enough to draw attention."

As we pulled out of town, I had to choose a direction. Leslie muttered a few strange words and the crystal pulled toward the northwest of the map. She followed the pull until it locked onto an invisible slot directly over the northeast corner of Washington State.

"Damn it…"

I turned down the road that would take us toward the nearest highway leading to where the crystal indicated.

Maybe if Madam Bina had been around after the events of Arkham, she could have gotten through to Leslie about all this magic and the dangers it posed. Someone close enough to the entity that pulled me out of the collapsing basement must have some idea of how all this madness worked. Instead, when we got to her storefront, I found an empty closet of a shop, which I don't even want to think about, and a letter. What was it with these people and their letters?

Dear Travis,

I hope Nyarlathotep was able to keep you safe. I've had to move my shop as a precaution in the event Mandeville sniffs out my involvement. He's always been a bit of a bastard. Who knew he'd try something like this, though?

Be careful, Travis. Settle your affairs in the city and disappear. You stopped Mandeville once, but he is resourceful and will hunt down <u>anyone</u> who may be of use.

I am going away for some time. I am sorry I won't be around to help you further.

I always liked you. A pity I couldn't say goodbye in person.

Bina

Something about the way she emphasized "anyone" made me think she suspected about Leslie but was being careful not to mention it outright. Or I was a victim of wishful thinking, not wanting to be the only other person burdened with the knowledge that the soul Mandeville lusted after was in my inept care.

It took two days of driving, broken up with short, six-hour spans of sleep found in cheap roadside motels, to reach the border of Washington. While stopped for gas, Leslie purchased another map. This one was for the state itself, and she repeated the trick with the crystal.

"There. In the Monashee Mountains. That's where we'll find the flower I need."

Very few roads offered access to the mountains. I should have waited and considered a better plan, but instead, exhausted and wishing this little scavenger hunt to be done, I pointed the car west and made for the Monashee Mountains.

As we drew close, the roads turned from asphalt to crushed stone, to packed dirt. When the dirt gave way to grass and moist, fertile ground, I stopped the car to avoid getting stuck. The Buick had been growling its displeasure with the off-road journey for the last hour, and my rear end agreed. The sun slid down the sky into night. I gauged we had maybe three hours of daylight left.

"Is it close? The Buick can't go any farther without risking getting bogged down and stuck out here."

Leslie consulted her map and shook her head. "We still have a decent amount of ground to cover before we can even start looking." She pointed ahead. "We need to go into the woods."

I saw the edge of the tree line at least a football field away and cursed. There was no way around it. We needed to gear up for a hike.

As I rummaged through the trunk of my car in search of canteens and flashlights—we'd stocked the car with all kinds of emergency necessities—Leslie smirked at the stream of grumbling bubbling out of my mouth. "Not the outdoorsy type?"

"When, in the last year, have I ever given you the impression I like the outdoors? I grew up in the city like a normal human being. The woods are for bears, deer, and criminals."

I found the canteens and flashlights after rearranging the entire back end of the car. "We'll need to find a stream or something to fill these up."

"Grab a couple iodine packets."

I nodded, found a small pile we'd purchased with the rest of the survival gear, and pocketed four packets.

According to her map, we faced a long hike before we would find the plant she needed.

"What are we looking for again?"

"*Cypripedium montanum*, better known as the white version of Yellow Lady's-Slippers. Worse, we need to find one suffused with magenta."

"So that's rare?"

"Like a five-leaf clover."

"Great."

Monashee Mountains

The sun set fast as we trudged through the woods searching for the flower Leslie needed to make us harder to notice and remember. She pointed out the yellow variety early on. There were whole clusters of them along our search. I thanked whatever powers that ruled with mercy in the universe when I spied a small gathering of white ones, but none had the necessary magenta accent.

Our pace slowed as night overtook the landscape. The thick canopy blotted out the moon and stars. I could just make out a nearly full moon through the breaks in foliage, but it did us little good.

"We should head back to the car and wait 'til morning," I suggested.

"No. We're close. I can feel it somehow." Leslie dropped to her knees and withdrew the crystal once more. She muttered another group of spidery words, and the crystal pulled in a specific direction. "Very close. Come on!"

Leslie dashed off into the darkness. I was able to follow the bouncing of her flashlight, but navigating the wild landscape proved more and more difficult as twilight faded into night. Every step I took felt like a nearby tree had shifted its roots to trip me.

"Leslie, slow down. Don't get too far ahead."

"Hurry up, old man!" She giggled from the shadows, but waved her flashlight ahead to make sure I could follow.

A small smile flashed over my lips despite my annoyance at her boundless energy and unyielding fearlessness. Even after everything she'd been through and studied, she remained upbeat and ready to take on the world. Had I been in her shoes, I would have crawled into a deep pit and whimpered myself to sleep only to wake up, dig deeper, and continue weeping for my lost future. Leslie believed there was a way out of our mess buried within the books taken from the Miskatonic University Library, and we only needed to stay ahead of Mandeville long enough to find it.

Her light vanished. I stopped breathing. Fear seized my senses. Maybe she had disappeared around a tree? A terrible, pain-filled scream tore through the woods.

"Leslie!" I raced onward, stumbling over more roots and kicking aside rocks. Leslie appeared in front of me; her flashlight lay on the ground facing a small growth of magenta suffused white flowers.

"Why'd you scream like that?"

"It wasn't me." Leslie pointed deeper into the woods. "It sounded like a child."

"Stay here!"

Without thinking, I charged deeper into the dark forest. Engulfed by the aroma of spruce, cedar, and hemlock, I pushed through stabbing branches, intent on helping a lost, possibly endangered, child. Crashing through the overgrowth, trampling everything and anything in my path, collecting bruises with each step, I heard a low growling under the piercing shriek of the child. A clearing, bathed in moonlight, appeared within the crush of trees. An enormous creature covered in thick fur thrashed at a small child cowering at the base of a wide tree. The creature's shadow covered the child, but I could see the streaks of blood gliding through the air and splashing across bark and leaves with each strike.

I dropped the flashlight, withdrew my gun, and fired a shot into the air. The towering beast froze mid-swing. When it turned, my mouth dried, and my mind blanked. I stared into the golden eyes of an enormous bipedal wolf. Blood dripped from his long-clawed fingers. Its massive hands could wrap around my head with ease. Red drool lined its fanged jaw. The hunched monster turned and rose to its full height of seven or eight feet.

As I stared at the impossible beast, unable to rip my gaze away, I absorbed all the physical details without allowing it to touch deep inside where my executive mind considered each situation with cool detachment. It was all academic until the creature chuffed out a gruff chuckle. That single laugh broke me. Its features twisted into what could only be described as enraged amusement. Bloodlust reflected in the curling snarl while its eyes flashed with gleeful anticipation.

I lowered my gun from the sky and leveled it at the feral creature looming before me. Three shots roared in the natural silence of the night. The muzzle flash blinded me for a second as it lit up the darkness. When my eyes readjusted, the creature remained standing. It scratched at the area where I shot it as if relieving itself of a small itch. Those glowing yellow eyes turned toward me, filled with equal parts hate and hunger.

It crouched down, muscles tensed, ready to pounce. Without any other choice, I took aim, intending to die with only empty casings left in my revolver. Before either of us could make our moves, a howl resonated through the air. The beast perked up and peered into the darkness. A quick glance revealed another pair of golden eyes watching from a distance. The wolf forgot all about me and its previous victim and bounded into the woods. I returned my gun to its holster, picked up the flashlight, and shook off the encounter long enough to get to the child's side.

What lay before me, though a child, was not human. The beam from my flashlight revealed a small being covered in thick brown hair. It appeared to have human features mixed with those of a gorilla. I checked for a pulse but found nothing. Whatever it was, it had lost too much blood from the attack. Light footsteps rushed closer from where I had emerged into the clearing. Leslie broke free of the foliage, her eyes filled with worry.

"I heard the shots. Are you ok?"

"No. I have no idea what I just saw nor whatever this is." I waved at the body.

Leslie inched closer but froze when she saw the strange, youthful features. "It's only a child. Is it dead?"

"Yes."

"I hope you killed the thing that did this."

I looked into her eyes, astonished by her forthright desire for vengeance. She stared down at the body, both in wonderment and shock. In that moment, I wasn't sure she even knew she'd spoken out loud.

"No, I shot at the monster attacking it. The bullets bounced off. Something called it away before it could do the same to me."

A low rumble, one we hadn't noticed at first, grew in strength. The woods trembled in response to the increasing power. I prayed the wolf-monster wasn't returning with a whole pack. If so, why did it run away only to return? My gun wasn't much more than a nuisance. A quick glance at Leslie gave me the strength to face down whatever sort of death rampaged our way.

"Run. I'll hold them off."

"I'm not leaving you, Travis."

"I promised—"

"Shut up! I don't care about your promise. I'd rather die here with you than keep running alone." The hurt in her eyes told me everything I needed to know. I nodded and aimed my revolver straight ahead. I had two more shots. I'd have to make them count if we were going to have any chance of escaping.

Monstrous, humanoid wolves did not burst from the woods slavering and grunting, all teeth and claws. Instead, full-grown, ten-foot-high versions of the dead child (or baby considering the size of the creatures in front of us) stampeded into view. They shattered massive, towering cedar trees, bashing them aside as if punching through cardboard. A thick cloud of wild musk flooded the clearing. Within the head-shaped nest of hair and twigs, the clearest blue eyes stared out with undeniable intelligence. I counted five of the creatures but sensed a horde of them hidden within the inner depths of the woods.

"It wasn't us!" It was the only thing I could think to say.

The hairy giant at the front of the group noticed the smaller body at the base of the spruce and gasped. It's a strange thing to hear a creature that shouldn't exist gasp in horrified surprise. A different member of the group choked as a human might on their sorrow. Another emitted a low growl. Of the three distinct reactions, the growl was the one that spread to the others, both seen and hidden.

I raised my revolver and aimed at the lead creature. "Please, understand me. We didn't do this."

The five giants stalked forward, either not understanding or not caring, clenching their boulder-like fists as if they already had us by the throat. I fired one shot over the leader's head, close enough to singe its dirt crusted fur. It didn't flinch. Without recourse, I fired again. The second bullet hit center mast. A trail of blood tickled down the monster's fur-knotted chest. It stopped and peered down. With a delicate touch, it dug into the small hole and pulled the bullet free. Blood spurted, then flowed from the wound, but the creature remained standing. It examined the pathetic lump of lead in its enormous grasp before flicking it aside and unleashing a deafening roar. The horde in the depths added their voices to the leader's rage, shaking the forest.

"We need to run." I pushed the revolver back into the holster and snapped the leather strap secure with the fluidity of habit as I retreated from the horde's vocal assault.

Leslie stepped forward, face locked in concentration. "Cover your eyes," she said. I reached for her, but the air had turned thick with energy. Her hand shot forward as she spoke a single word. Echoing with power, her voice came out distorted. A blast of light exploded all around us. I managed to cover my eyes and turn away, but not fast enough.

Once I'd blinked the searing pain from my eyes, I still had trouble seeing through the after images burned into my vision. All the creatures had fallen back or to the ground, rubbing and clawing at their eyes. I searched for Leslie as my vision continued to clear, feeling along the ground as much as seeing past the combination of ghostly images and natural darkness. My foot caught against some kind of mound. At first, I suspected a large root, but it was too soft.

I found Leslie crumped on the ground, unconscious and struggling to breathe. Scooping her into my arms, her weakened heartbeats whispered against my chest as short and shallow wheezes fluttered past slack lips. Off balance and desperate, I trampled through the thick brush without the assistance of light or any real idea of direction. Behind me, a chorus of rage and sadness erupted. The ground beneath my feet vibrated with their shared distress. Whether they were chasing after or bellowing their frustration into the world, I couldn't allow myself to speculate. My only concern in those blurred moments was to get Leslie to the car and then to a doctor as soon as possible.

I'm not sure how I got out of those woods, but when I broke free of the tree line and found my Roadster standing in the middle of an empty field, I almost wept. My legs were jelly, my arms burned from carrying Leslie, and my brain hurt from everything I had just witnessed. I eased Leslie into the passenger seat and stumbled around to the driver's side. One last glance at the forest froze me in place. A swarm of piercing blue eyes stared out from the depths of the woods. If they decided to come after us, there was no guarantee we would outrun them.

They remained within the confines of the forest, unable or unwilling to step out into the open. I eased into the driver's seat and soon we were coasting down the dirt hillside, then over packed stone, and finally onto the asphalt roads away from the creature-infested mountain and forest. Once I was certain we weren't being followed, I pulled over and tore open the map Leslie had used to find the mountain. Under the light of the moon, the map showed a hospital due west in a town called Oroville. I tossed the map aside and hit the road hard. I kept checking behind us and on both sides. Any flicker of movement in the night made me jump, expecting a ten-foot, hairy giant to come bounding into us. Even made of steel, I wasn't confident the car would survive an encounter with whatever we'd escaped.

Hell, I knew we hadn't escaped. They let us go. The question became why?

With Leslie struggling to breathe in the seat next to me, I couldn't bring myself to care either way.

Oroville, Washington

When we pulled up to the small-town hospital, a thought occurred to me. *What the hell was I going to say?* I slid to a stop
in front of the main entrance, jumped out, and ran around to
the passenger side to lift Leslie out of the car. I kicked at the
front door until someone came to investigate the noise. After
the on-duty nurse saw us, the annoyance on her face melted
into alarm. She yelled for assistance and held the door open as
I rushed inside.

"What happened?" the nurse asked.

"We were out... stargazing... and she fainted."

"Does she have a history of that sort of thing?"

"Not that I know of."

"Are you her father?"

"No."

The nurse cocked a judgmental eyebrow at me.

"I'm her guardian, lady. Now help her."

She scoffed, rushing off to find a doctor when another nurse
appeared rolling a wheelchair into the lobby. I eased Leslie into
the chair and followed as they brought her to the nearest available
examination room. Leslie's eyes fluttered as if she were struggling
to come out of a deep sleep. Her lips quivered to speak, but she was

still far too weak. The doctor entered and scanned over a chart the nurse must have filled out while tracking him down.

"I'm Dr. Oyacken. Can you tell me what happened?"

He was middle-aged with dark hair and light brown skin. He tried to look amiable, but there was a sternness to his general demeanor. He radiated what people might call gravitas. I wanted to tell him the whole truth without hesitation but kept my common sense in check.

"We were out for a late-night hike when we came across a hungry pack of wolves. We're not from around here and had never seen wolves that big. I think she passed out from the shock."

"You told the nurse…" He checked the notes scribbled onto the chart. "'Stargazing'?"

"You have to hike to find a good spot to star-gaze."

"Of course."

Same as the nurse, Oyacken assumed I was a lecher. "Listen, can you help her? I'm worried she may be seriously injured."

He nodded and used a stethoscope to listen to her breathing then a small, tube-like tool with a large, flat black circle atop to examine her eyes as he eased them open. After making some notes, he smiled, "She seems to be suffering from extreme exhaustion. Must have been a vigorous hike."

"Now, listen—"

"I'm not here to judge, sir. She'll be fine. She just needs rest and food when she wakes up." Oyacken touched the clipboard under his arm. "Where did you say you were hiking?"

"I didn't. I don't even know if the place has a name. It was east of here, up a mountain, in some woods. She wanted to see if she could find some rare plant, as well. Yellow Slippers or something, but white with magenta highlights."

Oyacken paused and uttered a strange word with a hushed reverence and fear before asking, "The Monashee Mountains?"

"Maybe. I'd have to look at a map."

"How big were those wolves you saw?"

"Bigger than I'd ever seen before, but what do I know? I'm from the city."

"Right, of course," Oyacken said. "That makes sense. And you only saw wolves? Nothing else?"

I stared him straight in the eyes, trying to discern how much *he* knew, how much *I* should reveal, and how much to trust him. "Yes," I said. Assuming what I'd seen wasn't entirely a secret, it was enough of one that those in the know tiptoed around it. "You whispered something earlier. I didn't quite catch it."

"Hmm? Oh, nothing. An old tribal word from when I was younger and living on the reservation."

"Oyacken is a tribal name?"

"No. It was just easier to accept colonial names for the census takers than fight a losing battle. The same happened to those hopeful immigrants on Ellis Island when they came here, and it'll happen to many more. Immigrant or native doesn't seem to matter to those in power." He sighed, tired of discussing a long-debated topic. "There are greater battles to fight."

"What was your ancestral name?"

Leslie mumbled something which brought our attention around to her.

"What did she say?" Oyacken asked.

We leaned in. "Didn't kill the baby. Wolf. Please, listen..."

"She's delirious," I said. I was too tired to think of anything better.

"Naturally." Oyacken considered me for a moment. "You said you're not from around here? Do you have a place to stay?"

"Not yet."

"I can suggest a place further south in Tonasket, the Whitestone Hotel. I'll call ahead for you. One of our doctors just moved down there to open a practice if your friend needs to be seen again. The town is far from the forests connected to the Monashee Mountains."

We stared at one another for a beat, leaving much left unsaid. To be honest, I didn't want to know. As soon as Leslie was up and around, we were high-tailing it away from those mountains. I'd head straight to Mexico if I didn't think we'd stand out that far south. "Appreciate it, Doc. What do I owe you?"

Oyacken squeezed out one more smile. "Don't worry about it. I didn't have to do anything other than reassure you. Just help your friend here to heal up and go south to Tonasket. Tonight. Good evening, sir." A nurse appeared at the door to assist me with getting Leslie back to the car.

Oyacken wanted us not only out of his hospital but also out of his town and far from the forest. I had the sinking feeling he wasn't as worried about our well-being as his own. His reaction to the revelation of our being in the Monashee Mountains set him on edge. Whether he was more concerned about the wolves or the humanoid creatures whose young had been hurt, I couldn't tell.

Maybe it was both, and he just wanted anyone who was embroiled between them out of his town.

Once Leslie was secured in the passenger seat, I got back in the car and headed south toward Tonasket.

Whitestone Hotel

It didn't take much searching to locate the Whitestone Hotel, a large building surrounded by a sea of squat ones. The street was deserted, so I was able to park right at the entrance. Leaving Leslie in the car, I entered the main lobby and found an old man standing half-asleep at the desk.

"Hey, wake up. I need a room."

The old clerk opened his eyes with the slowness of a glacier and scanned me up and down. "You the ones Dr. Oyacken called about?"

"Yeah."

"Where's your girlfriend?"

"She's not my girlfriend... Buddy, you have a room for us or not?"

"Sure, I put aside the honeymoon suite for you two."

"Old man, I am way too tired for this. One room. Two beds. How much?"

"A dollar a night. Need help with any bags?"

"No. Just give me the key. I'll take care of the bags after I get some sleep." I slapped a five on the counter as the old man pulled a room key from the rack behind him.

Outside, I opened the passenger door and nudged Leslie to see if she could be roused to walk on her own. She glanced around, unsure or unable to make sense of her surroundings. I guided her out of the car, trying to reassure her with low whispers. She relaxed and allowed me to guide her forward. Her feet shuffled and slid across the lobby floor. The stairs were too much, so I ended up carrying her the rest of the way to our room.

In the bed, Leslie curled up under the covers and drifted off into another deep sleep. I stood over her, watching for any sign she might be injured or in distress. Every breath came soft and natural. I fell back onto my own bed and exhaled the mountain of stress I'd carried on my shoulders since we fled from Illinois. Leslie hated this life on the run, separated from everyone and everything on the suspicion that a stray word would filter back to New York and Mandeville. I was used to being alone, but this was different, and I didn't like the rudderless existence we now shared. But what choice did we have? If Mandeville found out she was alive, he would hunt her down for whatever dark purpose he had planned. At some point, as all these concerns roiled through my mind, sleep found me.

The next morning, I woke to find Leslie missing. I jumped up and ran into the hallway.

She stepped out of the common bathroom down the hall and smiled. While my heart slowed to the mild rate of a Tommy gun on the verge of overheating, I asked, "How're you feeling?"

"Better. I think I was just over exhausted after... you know." She extended a fist in front of her and opened her fingers like an explosion. "What'd I miss?"

"Not much. Chased through the woods by enormous beasts. A sea of piercing blue eyes staring at me from the darkness. Raced through the night to find you a hospital." I guided her back into the room. I didn't think there was anyone else renting a room, but there was no reason to risk sounding like raving lunatics to eavesdroppers. "The doctor who treated you got cagey when I mentioned wolves and where we were."

Leslie padded down the hallway and whispered, "You told him what you saw?"

"Not exactly. I just said we ran across some big wolves, and you fainted."

"Thanks!"

I closed the door and locked it. "Well, I wasn't going to say you passed out after casting a spell to ward off a horde of giant beast-men who probably wanted to kill us."

"I guess."

"I'm sorry. I'll try and be the one who faints next time."

"I'd appreciate it."

"Anyway, he started asking odd questions like how big the wolves were, did we see anything else? And then firmly suggested we drive an hour south to this hotel because it was farther from any of the woods connect to Monashee. He was adamant we not stay in Oroville."

"What is going on around here?"

"No idea, and I don't want to know. We should get the hell out of the area as soon as possible."

"Sure, but I want to try that shielding spell first. If it works, no one should be able to notice me unless I let them. It should make it impossible, or at least very difficult, for my uncle to find me."

"Are you sure you should do that after last night? That spell knocked you out cold."

"I was rushed and didn't focus. I'll be ok now. I just need to concentrate."

"Leslie, maybe—"

"Travis, I'm doing this. I don't want to keep looking over my shoulder forever. I need to try this." It was the first time I witnessed the desperation weighing her down. Her whole being radiated the kind of fear that breaks even the hardest souls. Still, she stood against the madness of last night and refused to shrink away from the magic that held both answers and unknown costs.

"Fine. Let's head down to the car and get our things. I paid for five nights, so we may as well relax for a bit while we can."

Once we hauled our belongings up the stairs, Leslie didn't pause to take a shower and change into fresh clothes. Instead, she tore through her bottomless bag. One after another, withered objects, dried out plants, and one book made a small pile on a simple desk pushed up against the wall opposite her bed. After some searching, she found a folded handkerchief containing the flowers she'd collected the previous night.

"I was only able to harvest enough for one of us before everything went crazy. If this works, we'll go and get more." Before I could object, she held up her hand. "From a different forest, of course. I'm not insane."

I chose not to argue the point as she readied the components for the spell. Her current course of action reinforced my opinion she walked a fine line between restraint and recklessness.

She began piling everything into her arms. "I need a bowl of water. Help me carry all this to the bathroom down the hall. I can use the sink."

I picked up most of her components, unwilling to touch the book. Memories of how some of the other books felt back in Arkham still crawled under my fingertips and through my dreams. In the bathroom, she filled the sink with water and began mixing in the components while reciting the spell in a language she'd cobbled together from her eldritch books. I never asked about it and often wished she'd never worked it out. She took the White Lady's Slippers from the handkerchief, stirred the petals into the water, and chanted a command. Her voice hummed low and distinct. The magenta of the flowers drained away, staining the water. A similar glow rose from the concoction, and the scent of spring filled the bathroom.

She dipped her hand into the water and came up with a small pool trapped in her palm. She came over to me and dabbed a finger in the water. "Close your eyes." I did. Her fingers painted water over my eyelids and a faint glow of magenta suffused the darkness before dissipating. "Done. Now, if you don't mind, I need to wash my body with the water."

Heat exploded up my neck and over my face. "Right. Of course. I'll just be back in the room when you're done." I turned away to make my escape but stopped. Pointing at my eyes, I asked, "Will this make it so I can see you?"

"According to the book, yeah."

"What if someone recreates the spell?"

"No. It would have to be this particular water, which I will be draining as soon as I'm done. Also, I'll be chanting your name as I'm washing myself."

The thought made me queasy. I left the bathroom and waited to hear her lock the door before retreating to my room. After unpacking our clothes, I put everything away in the worn dresser across from my bed. I was about to strap on my holster when Leslie returned, her hair damp and last night's clothes clinging to her body. I dropped my gun and holster into the drawer and pointed to the fresh change of clothes I'd arranged for her. She'd shown me how to retrieve items from her bag. It always felt like shoving my hand into a humid pit stuffed with cotton. I hated it.

"Figured you'd want something clean."

"Definitely." She squeezed my arm in thanks, aware of my aversion to reaching into her bag. "I just have to wait for the potion to air dry. If I wipe it away with a towel, it won't take."

Before I could answer, a heavy knock popped through the door. No matter where you are in the country, you can always recognize the police at your door by the way they knock. I waved Leslie away from the door. "Yes?"

"Travis Daniels? This is Sheriff Praswá of the Okanogan Police Department. I'm here about your attack last night and the murder your... associate mentioned. Open up."

Sheriff Praswá

Praswá strolled in and completed a quick survey of the room. Leslie had taken a seat on the edge of the bed as close to one of the corners as possible. His eyes passed over her without a second's hesitation. I remained impassive as the effects of her spell proved to be powerful. No reason to drag her into this if it could be avoided.

"What's all this about a murder?"

"The doc up in Oroville said your friend mentioned a child murder up in the Monashee Mountains. He was concerned and gave me a call. Told me where to find you."

"That was helpful of him, but I don't know anything about a murder, Sheriff."

Praswá gave the room another look, checking all the corners but one. "And where is your associate?"

"She's out for a walk. She needed some fresh air after her ordeal last night."

"Yes, you told Oyacken you were attacked by a pack of wolves?"

"No, I said big wolves."

Praswá smiled. "My mistake. Big wolves. Then your companion..."

I remained silent.

"She mumbled something about a baby who'd been killed?"

"Delirium."

"Well, her delirium proved correct."

What the hell? Is he about to tell me they found that creature's body and are now investigating?

"I had the forest rangers check the area. They found your car's tracks, followed your path into the woods, and discovered the clearing where we presume you were attacked. You weren't subtle in your escape. Broken saplings and tree limbs everywhere, I'm told."

"Big wolves."

"They found signs of an attack and blood everywhere. Why don't you tell me what you saw."

"Big wolves."

"Now, listen. We can either have a polite discussion here or I can haul you down to the deputy's station in town."

I stood silent. If I told the guy the truth, he'd throw me into an asylum and Leslie would be on her own. If he sweated me in whatever backwater closet this town had for a substation, he'd have to let me go eventually. No body, no crime.

"Have it your way. Travis Daniels, you're under arrest for trespassing on government property. You have the right..." His words faded into the din of a thousand detectives reciting my rights over the years—every time I refused to give up a client or turn over a source. I resisted looking in Leslie's direction as he led me out. I didn't dare direct his attention to her. "Can I at least leave a note for my friend to sit tight while you waste both our time?"

"Shut up. You can tell the clerk at the front desk on the way out."

I thanked whatever friendly powers still existed in the universe for stopping me from strapping on my gun. That would have brought far too many questions and possibly gotten it lost in the evidence room. Praswá pushed me into his car and drove me around a few blocks until we reached a small building with a red brick front, two large windows, and the word "HARDWARE" painted in large block letters above two bright white doors. To the left of the main entrance, added as a kind of afterthought, was a dirty, worn, white door with the word "DEPUTY" painted in gold on the dingy glass. I couldn't tell if the store was open or not.

"Nice place you got here."

"Never needed much else. We have a quiet town."

"Everyone does until they don't, sheriff."

He scoffed and got out. Once we were inside the substation, I was planted in a chair in front of the only desk while Praswá took a seat across from me. A layer of dust had settled over the room.

"You guys don't get much use of this room, do you?"

"I'm not normally up this way. I try and stay in Okanogan. I only get called up here for serious matters."

"Like trespassing?"

"Like murder, smart-ass."

I shrugged.

"I made some calls before I came to get you. Talked to some people out in New York. You're a long way from home, Mr. Daniels."

"Decided to see the country." How much had he said on the phone to people out east? The wrong words in the wrong ears would be trouble for us. We needed to get the hell out of this town.

"Some of your old friends implied you were in debt to the wrong people and ran."

"Old news. I paid what I owed on my way through the city. I'm free and clear."

"No one's heard from you for nearly a year. You've just been traveling all this time?"

"Pretty much."

"Until you ran across some 'big wolves' and happened to flee from a clearing where there's evidence of violence and enough blood to assume something died."

"If you say so."

Praswá stared me down, but that sort of nonsense doesn't work on anyone but the nervous and guilty. The only things I did shoot at, unsuccessfully, were two monsters before running for our lives.

"The ranger also found six discharge bullets in or near the clearing. Know anything about that?"

"Big wolves."

No reason to deny I fired my weapon. Who wouldn't when attacked by wild animals? Praswá could see he wasn't going to get anywhere with me. For a brief second, I thought he was about to say something crazy. There was a glint in his eye that suggested he knew I was lying but wasn't sure how much I'd seen or knew. He settled back into his chair. "Mr. Daniels, if you don't tell me everything, there's very little I can do to help you."

I couldn't help but laugh. "Sheriff, there's nothing you can do to help me. I am down a very dark river without a paddle. The last thing I want is to drag some well-intentioned soul into hell with me."

"But you'll drag a young woman with you?"

There wasn't anything to say that wouldn't put him and us into greater danger. Something supernatural was happening in the town, and I knew more than ever, Leslie and I needed to clear out before we got caught up in it any further.

"Listen, I'm sorry if I trespassed. I didn't see any signs. If you're going to fine me, do it."

"I ought to lock you up until you start talking—" Praswá looked out the window behind me and stopped cold. He jumped up and headed for the door. "Don't move."

I turned to see him exit the building and cross the street to confront an honest-to-god tribesman wearing hand-stitched leather clothes, sitting horseback with no saddle, waiting in the middle of the road. The horseman spoke down to Praswá, who in turn argued back. The horseman didn't seem moved by Praswá's retort and rode off. Praswá stared across the road into an empty field, kicked at a clump of dirt in the road, and came back. I turned away without speaking.

Praswá returned to his chair. His face was a deep, angry red. He looked me over, measuring me against whatever had gone on outside. When he leaned forward, his words came out through gritted teeth. "You're free to go."

I stood and turned to leave. I wanted to ask for a ride back to the hotel but decided that would be pushing my luck. As I walked out the door, he said, "I strongly suggest you leave town, Daniels. You have no idea the storm that's brewing around here."

I nodded to his reflection in the glass and stepped out.

Colville Reservation

Packed-dirt streets carved paths, defining plots of land through Tonasket. Residential homes peppered a vast scrubland divided into large rectangles ready for homes to be built. The air swirled with dust and dried brush. Small towns throughout the west were nothing like the cities and towns of the northeast I'd known most of my life. This was a world that had the space to expand yet refused to do so. One could sit back and see the potential all around. Many who lived and loved in such towns didn't want the bustle of the larger cities. They wanted the open spaces and vast silence. To me, the quiet made me uneasy, as if something were waiting beyond my senses, ready to pounce.

The downtown area contained small buildings, both brick and wood, clustered together. They were nothing like the groupings found in even the smallest borough of New York but still packed together for strength, holding up each other to fend off the larger corporations who were taking greater and greater interest in frontier towns. By the number of lumber yards in and around the town, it wasn't difficult to work out which business was dictating these people's lives. But for the number of lumber yards and sawmills, there was a distinct lack of sawdust and activity for a weekday. As I passed storage facilities, they laid wide open and barren of product.

I found my way back to Whitcomb Ave and entered the Whitestone. The clerk perked up as I entered and waved me down.

"I never saw your companion return, sir. I do hope she's ok?"

It took me a minute to remember what I'd said earlier. "Oh, don't worry. She's very capable. I'm sure everything is fine. Thanks."

He nodded as I took the stairs up. Leslie was in the room, leaning over her books again. "We need to get out of this place," I said.

Leslie glanced up. "What? Do they think we had something to do with the murder?"

"First of all, animals can't murder animals. Neither can monsters for that matter. It's just nature. Second, he doesn't think we were involved, but he knows something. The doctor called the sheriff, and both seem fixated on the woods, the wolves, and whatever else I may have seen. They seem to expect me to admit to seeing the other monsters, but don't want to ask outright. Then, some tribesman came by, had words with the sheriff, and I was set free. Something odd is going on in this place, and I don't want anything to do with it."

"I think we should help."

"Are you serious?"

"Yes! We witnessed a child get mauled to death. Those creatures were angry and scared. They saw one of their children dead and lashed out. They aren't monsters, and I want to help them find the thing that attacked their child."

"Didn't you learn your lesson back in Arkham? Getting involved will bring the wrong kind of attention."

"I'm protected now."

"I'm not!"

Leslie slammed the book she was reading closed and stormed out of the room. I figured I'd let her cool off and started packing our things, intent on being ready to leave when she returned. I strapped on my holster, feeling naked without it. Even driving across the vast expanses of American farmlands under endless blue skies felt wrong without the constant pressure against my ribs. I hated driving through those places, so big and open. It made me realize how small I was in the grand tapestry of life. A chuckle slipped out. Thoughts like that never crossed my mind back when I traveled through the cramped streets of the city. Back when things were simple.

When I carried my suitcase down the stairs to put in my car, I found Leslie standing just outside the front door speaking to a man. The window was coated with dirt, making it impossible to see who she was with. I rushed forward. Outside, I recognized the man as the one on the horse outside the deputy's office.

"Can I help you?" I asked.

Leslie saw the suitcase and grimaced. She stepped over and snatched it out of my hand. "We're not leaving." Before I could argue, she proceeded inside and carried the luggage back upstairs.

"Leslie!" I shouted after her.

"She is correct. You cannot leave."

I turned toward the man. "And you are?"

He looked off into the distance as if searching for the answer. "You must come to speak with the elder."

"Listen, buddy, I'm not speaking to anyone else. The sheriff said I should get gone, and once I get my suitcase back, I'm dragging it and that girl out of town."

The man didn't react. He kept staring out across the empty lots of dirt and clear blue sky. The faint hint of a smile seemed to curl at the corners of his lips, but his stoic mask made me second guess what I glimpsed stirring under the surface.

"You have witnessed a darkness. The elder has questions. You must come with me." The man stepped out into the packed-dirt road. I hadn't noticed the horse waiting across the street until just then. He strode up, took the horse's reins, and leapt up. It was the most graceful maneuver I'd ever seen. For a moment, the man appeared to be a ballet dancer floating under the power of invisible wings. I expected an orchestra to swell into existence and play along to his smooth, practiced movements.

"We need to follow him." Leslie marched past me and got into the car. The man waited in the center of the road, staring straight ahead.

"Damn it."

We followed behind the man for miles, heading south. By the time we got to the Colville Reservation, most of the day had passed and the sun hung low to the west. Leslie remained sullen and silent the entire drive. I wanted to talk sense into her, but as the words bubbled up in my mind, I felt the anger and frustration of trying to keep her alive and safe darken my words. No matter what I said or did, she continued to go out of her way to put herself in danger.

Instead of igniting a fight, I chose to remain silent as we crept along behind the man on his horse.

When we entered the small town of Omak, a field of fruit trees covered the surrounding landscape. The man rode on until we came to a ranch bursting with herds of roaming cattle, bays full of snorting pigs, and squawking chicken coops. I parked near what I took for the main residence and got out. The man on his horse indicated with a single wave of his hand we should go to the front door before riding off.

The door rattled under the weight of my knocking, but it didn't seem ready to fall away from the hinges just yet. A young boy opened the door and stared at us without speaking.

I've never known how to talk to children. Treating them like tiny adults didn't always work and would sometimes result in evil looks from those around. Leslie crouched down in front of the boy and smiled. "Hi, how are you? We were told someone wanted to talk to us."

The boy raced back into the shadows of the house. The shuffle of feet approached soon after. An old man waved in greeting and motioned for us to enter. We were shown to a kitchen table, offered seats, and soon had strong, black coffee in front of us. It smelled wonderful and tasted even better.

"Thanks. It's been ages since I've had a good cup of coffee."

The old man took his seat and nodded. He took a sip from his own cup and leaned back to get a good look at us.

"Tell me about the wolf you saw that killed the child."

The matter-of-fact statement threw me off. There was no uncertainty or guile in his voice. He knew what had happened and could somehow ignore Leslie's spell as he took his time examining us both for reactions. He took another sip of coffee and seemed to accept the surprise washing over my face as a kind of confirmation.

I mentally retreated to the deputy's office and repeated as if an automaton, "Big wolf."

The elder chuckled. "Yeah, I'm sure it was. They look real big when they stand on two legs."

I leaned forward and placed my hands flat on the table to resist the urge raging through me to pull my gun and start shooting. It was Arkham all over again.

"Who are you?" I asked.

"Elder Alex Chelahitsa. I won't worry you over my Okanogan name. You are Travis Daniels, and she is Leslie Owens. Our spirit guardian has spoken of you."

Leslie gasped with panic while my hand twitched closer to my jacket. "How?" she asked.

"Hmm? Oh, your involvement with this situation brought you to our attention. We have already agreed to strengthen your cloak with some of our own magics to help you avoid detection from those who can... see around the spell by searching from different angles."

The disappointment on her face stabbed at my heart. I wanted to comfort her, but at the same time, it was a useful lessen in not relying on the magic she insisted was the answer to giving us an edge. There were no such things as easy answers or miracles. Worse, there was no way we could ever know as much about all this as Mandeville and using it always brought the risk of discovery.

Maybe we lucked out if this Elder had a way of strengthening her protections.

"How do you know our names? Did your spirit run a background check on us as well?"

"We heard about the incident in the woods from the doctor and learned the rest through word of mouth and preternatural means. We have quite a tight-knit community for one so spread out." Chelahitsa leaned forward and patted Leslie's hand. "Be calm. Our medicine doctor is already preparing you another layer of cloaking that should help hide you from the dark powers hunting you. The magics you used are dark in nature and come at a great cost. I urge you to resist their lure."

Leslie swallowed and nodded. Her eyes were wrapped in tears on the verge of release. My hand flinched for a different reason, but still I resisted the urge to provide comfort.

"What can you tell me of the wolf you saw?"

"Other than what you already seem to know?"

"Color, scars, anything unique. I know how that sounds under the circumstances."

"It was dark. Its eyes were golden and reflected like a cat's might. I couldn't make out the color of the fur. The thing was wild with rage and easily distracted. A complete lack of focus in who or what it was attacking."

"Interesting. Not one of ours, then."

"I'm sorry, one of yours?"

Chelahitsa sighed and eased out of his chair. "Come with me. You are far too involved not to be shown the truth. Perhaps you can be of assistance."

History and Mysticism

We were led deeper into the house to a room stacked with papers, books, documents, maps, and artifacts. Chelahitsa offered Leslie the only other chair in the room as he made his way around a cluttered desk to his own plush chair. He cleared an area at the center of his desk, sifted through a pile of scrolls in a small basket, and began unrolling them, one by one, on top of each other. There were crude illustrations of large beasts, some resembling wolves, and others, gorillas. Humans and forests, battles and peace talks, appeared across the sheets.

"When the Okanogan Tribe of the Sylix Nation roamed these lands, crossing the yet-to-be-declared border of the United States and Canada, we hunted and fished with the seasons, living out the winters in established locations. It was a peaceful existence." He allowed the first scroll to roll back up and reveal the one beneath.

"A great quake shook the lands to the north, driving all manner of creatures south. One such creature was the sc̓xʷanʕáytm̓,[1] now known as Sasquatch or Bigfoot. These wild men from the north entered the forests and mountains of our lands and took up

---

1. Wild Men, sasquatch, Bigfoot. Pronounced: schwän·ĀY·tem.

residence. Our people did not know what to make of these new creatures. To our great shame, we assumed they were a kind of bear and hunted them.

"A war ignited. They were relentless in their vengeance and swarmed down from the mountains, through the forests. We were pursued all the way back to our winter homes. In desperation, our medicine doctors begged the spirits of the earth and sky for reprieve. Only one answered. Our strongest were infused with the spirit of the wolf and changed before our eyes.

"The change drove them into a temporary madness. They fled into the forests, away from their loved ones before the bloodlust and rage clouded their minds. Over time, our həɫn'cičn' i? t čl-čaɬ[2] grew into their power and confronted the sc̓xʷanʕáy'tm' and pushed them back.

"Eventually, our people discovered the sc̓xʷanʕáy'tm' were an intelligent tribe. We were horrified by our actions, worked to avoid further conflict, and made amends to them. We learned each other's languages and customs, beliefs and legends. We were more alike than different. They returned to their mountains and we to our nomadic cycle.

"An agreement was struck that we would stay out of the mountains and they out of the plains. The forest would be neutral ground, good for hunting and gathering for both our peoples. We would both work to protect the earth that serves as a cradle to our civilizations. That agreement has held for thousands of years." As he rolled the last scroll up, he placed it to the side.

---

2. Wolves of the Forest. Pronounced: hesth·ench·EE·chen ee- t tsl·tsäel.

"That agreement, that truce, is in danger now because of what happened on Monashee Mountain. If the sc̓xʷanʕáy̓tm̓ choose to attack, they will massacre thousands in the throes of their collective rage. They already chafe against the gluttony of the lumber companies denuding the forests. I must know what happened on that mountain and who is responsible. With that information, maybe this battle can be averted."

Unable to speak, struggling to absorb everything Chelahitsa revealed, I lacked the conviction to tell him I wasn't interested. That I wanted nothing to do with Sasquatch or həɬn̓cic̓n̓ i? t c̓lc̓aɬ.

Leslie regained her composure faster than I did. "We'll help you."

The look in her eyes melted the last of my resolve to stay out of the whole affair. "Fine. But, if I'm going to do this, I expect to be paid."

Chelahitsa smiled. "Of course, Mr. Daniels. I always intended to pay for your services."

"I should also warn you. If I find out it was one of your həɬn̓cic̓n̓, I won't lie for you."

"I wouldn't ask you to."

"Good." I glanced at Leslie. "Also, your medicine doctors need to reinforce her cloak, as you called it. If she's discovered here by the one she's hiding from, we're gone. I won't risk her to save your truce."

Chelahitsa stood and extended his hand. "Agreed." We shook hands, and he slid a thin envelope free from one of the piles on his desk. "To get you started."

Once I secured the envelope into my inside jacket pocket, I asked, "Where can I find your həłn'cicn' i? t čl'caʔ?"

Chelahitsa motioned for us to leave his office. "There are some elders of our tribe who remain within the borders of the reservation, but with how you describe the attack, it sounds as if a younger n'čicn'[3] is to blame. There is a small group, all younger warriors, who broke away from the main body of the tribe. They stalk the outskirts of the lumber company's operations. Speak to them."

"Should I use your name to ensure cooperation?"

"No, absolutely not. You'd do better to find another approach. They will refuse to speak to you if they suspect you mean to interfere or coerce them on my behalf."

"Fair enough."

Chelahitsa led us out of the house and waved down our friend from earlier, though without his horse this time. "xʷuy'st iʔ xixw'tm' kł X'aʔkʷilx."[4]

The man nodded and motioned for us to follow.

We came to a small hut. I could feel the humidity pulsing from the single opening. The man held the flap for Leslie. She crouched down and entered. He waved me through. "No," I said. "Being unseen won't help me with this investigation. Another time." The truth was, I had no desire to immerse myself in any form of magic or mysticism. Leslie felt comfortable, maybe even compelled, to try every possible way to find a path back to a normal life. I was old

---

3. Wolf. Pronounced: ench·EE·chen.

4. "Take the girl to the medicine doctor." Pronounced: hüoo·ye-ST ee- hee·who·tm Kl-·Klä·QUeelh.

enough to accept no such thing existed. Still, we allow the young their illusions.

The man shrugged and dropped the flap. A low chant undulated from the hut, growing louder with each repetition. Heat vapor formed a jet of warped air rushing skyward from a hole in the roof. I wanted to peek in and make sure Leslie was ok, but the man stood with his back to the opening like a statue made of steel barring any attempt at entry now that the ritual had begun. The same strange inexplicable amusement wafted off the man, yet nothing about his demeanor indicated anything of the sort.

The ceremony went on for close to an hour before the chanting subsided and Leslie stumbled out, drenched in sweat. I rushed forward and offered my arm so she might steady herself. She waved me away and took a deep breath, savoring the cool northeastern air which seemed to revitalize her.

"The heat was more oppressive than I expected. I stood up too fast. Got light-headed. I'll be fine." She offered a smile before walking toward the car. The medicine doctor, a middle-aged man, emerged from the hut. He watched as Leslie made slow progress.

"Will she be ok?" I asked.

The medicine doctor nodded. "She is protected. But for how long, I do not know. The forces searching for her are powerful. Though they believe she is gone, they have cast a wide net and may find her again. I sensed she is worried about one in particular, but there are many who desire what she can provide." He leveled hard, knowing eyes, locking me down with only his gaze. "Protect her. The universe turns on a razor's edge at the best of times. She is a weight that could split all of reality open." The medicine doctor turned away and walked off into the growing darkness. I had no idea how much of the day had passed.

"I should get back to town before it gets too dark. Thank you for guiding us here."

"Do you need help getting back?" The man didn't seem worried and had probably only asked out of politeness.

"No. The route isn't complicated. You have a good night."

The man nodded and walked off after the medicine doctor, neither in a rush nor at a casual pace. He seemed to know he would get to whatever destination he was meant to arrive at when it was time to get there. Late or early didn't seem to drive his actions, only intent.

I rushed after Leslie to catch up and helped her into the car. The ride back took us past sundown, and we pulled up next to the hotel well into evening. A half-moon hung high above us, pale and bright in a cloudless sky. Leslie had fallen asleep on the drive back. I roused her enough to avoid carrying her through the hotel lobby again.

In the room, she collapsed into the bed, asleep before her body hit the mattress. I smiled, adjusted the covers over her, and got myself ready for bed. It looked as if I had a busy day ahead come morning.

Sheriff Praswá's Office

Loud banging snatched sleep from me.

"What the hell?" I tripped toward the door as the thuds continued without pause. Leslie lay still, oblivious to the racket. "I'm coming! Cut it out!"

Sheriff Praswá stood there with a deputy positioned to his right. "Mr. Daniels, I need to ask you to come with me to answer some additional questions."

"It's early, Sheriff. Can I come by your hole-in-the-wall later?"

"I need to insist you come now. We'll be having this discussion at the station house in Okanogan. We'll give you a ride."

"You going to be giving me a ride back?"

"We'll see how things go."

I sighed. "Let me get some clean clothes, at least?" A quick motion at my rumpled shirt confirmed for the sheriff that I wasn't stalling or trying to mess with him. He nodded and stepped into the doorframe to keep an eye on me. I removed my slept-in dress shirt and undershirt, splashed some cologne on my underarms and neck to cover the smell of sweat—asking for a shower would have been pushing my luck—and pulled on clean clothes.

I didn't make a move to strap on my holster or even go near it, but Praswá motioned at it hanging from the desk chair. "Hand over the gun. We need to run some tests." There was no way around it. He seemed the type not to bother if he didn't already have a reason to ask. I could have demanded a warrant or even denied his request. Both options would result in court documents, judges, and possibly news filtering back to New York. I needed to do whatever necessary to avoid that. If I cooperated, maybe I'd get it back sooner than later. I lifted the harness without touching the holster and handed it over.

"Where's the girl? Still out for that walk?"

My eyes never left his. "She's an early riser. You must have just missed her." If I glanced in Leslie's direction, it could guide his attention onto her.

"Sure. Must have slipped past the front desk unnoticed again, as well." Praswá glanced around the small room. "The desk attendant swears she's never left the building since you two checked in."

"He must be one hell of an employee to be working twenty-four straight hours without a break. How much they paying him?"

"Enough. Time to go."

I shrugged and fastened the last button on my shirt. Once I wedged my feet into my shoes, we were off.

The two officers flanked me all the way out of the hotel where they assisted me into the back seat of their car. We rumbled south along the same road I'd taken to Omak. We even passed through the small reservation town. As we glided past Chelahitsa's ranch, I could have sworn I saw the man with the horse standing out by the front gate, watching me pass. As I turned to confirm, the scene disappeared in the cloud of dust kicked up from the road.

We pulled into Okanogan, another small town, though the biggest of those I'd recently encountered. Defined by more packed-dirt roads, wooden buildings lined both sides of every street like mismatched toy blocks. Some of the buildings were larger than those in Tonasket, but the town had the same feel.

Praswá pulled up to a station house and escorted me inside. He showed me to a chair in front of a desk covered in pools of paper and stacked files. I managed to scan some of the pages before he pulled them all together and slapped a stray file on top. The town seemed to be having an epidemic of vandalism if the reports were to be believed.

"Sir?" A different deputy rushed over with a handful of messages.

"Not now, Simmons."

"But it's the local farmers. They are reporting a lot of missing cattle. Four different farms so far and a total of ten cows."

"Fine, just put the messages on the top of the pile. I'll get to it."

As Simmons rushed back to his deck, Praswá opened a different file with my fingerprints in black-and-white right on top.

"You got those fast."

Praswá sat, pulled my gun from its holster, popped the cylinder, and ejected the cartridges into an empty ashtray. He handed the tray to his deputy. "Get those to Jenkins. I want to know if they match the bullets found by the rangers."

"I told you I fired at the wolves."

Praswá flashed me a look that shut my mouth. Something more was going on. The deputy glanced from his boss to me and back before scampering off to follow orders.

"I don't want to hear a word out of you," Praswá said. "I told you to get out of town. Now, I've got to deal with this whole mess without setting off any number of small wars in the process."

"Sorry, but your friend on the horse invited me to speak with Elder Chelahitsa who in turn hired me to get to the bottom of what happened in—"

"I said shut your mouth." Praswá looked ready to leap across the table. "You think I'm worried about your 'big wolves'?" The sweat on his brow at their mere mention confirmed he was. "I've got a bigger issue brewing that threatens every town up and down the Great Northern Railway line. People's jobs are in danger if the logging operation's equipment keeps getting sabotaged. Most already hate the Colville Tribes here, and all they need is one solid reason to start lashing out. I'm not about to give them one."

"I'm sure I didn't just hear the suggestion that you'd ignore information regarding the recent spate of vandalism my company has suffered because you don't like the evidence?"

The speaker had somehow drifted into the room without either of us noticing. The impish man stood only three feet away from us, dressed in a neat, charcoal grey suit and holding a shiny, leather valise at his side. Intense boredom pulled at his soft features.

"Of course not, counselor. I will arrest whomever I discover is behind the sabotage, but they will have their day in a court of law. I won't have vigilante justice threaten *any* community."

"Good to hear."

"What brings you in? I've had all progress on the case couriered over to your offices."

"I have received the scant reports, thank you. No, I am here to secure Mr. Daniel's immediate release."

"What?" Both Praswá and I regarded the man as if he'd wandered into a bar holding a banana like a gun and requested everyone hand over their wallets.

He stepped up beside me unbidden and extended his hand. "Mr. Daniels, my name is Nathaniel Probst." I took his cold, dry hand. It felt as if my own internal warmth was being sucked out. I gave his arm one shake and let go, clenching warmth back into my fingers. "I represent Radiant Futures' interests in the area, and Mr. Olesk has expressed his intention to intercede on your behalf. Would that be satisfactory?"

Praswá began arguing and demanding Probst to leave, but the lawyer stood his ground and calmly argued his right to be there until I had made my decision. "Why does Mr. Olesk care about me?"

"He heard a private detective was in town and wished to... supplement... local law enforcement's efforts in uncovering who is behind the vandalism causing distress to our operations."

"I don't need some big-city detective nosing around and twisting up my investigation."

"I doubt he'll be too disruptive to your... efforts." Probst tried to smile. "Also, it will free you up to look into the cattle going missing. I hear many disappeared in the night."

"How did you—?"

"We've employed many of the local farmers to assist in repairing our equipment on site."

"How did you find out I was even in town, Mr. Probst?" I asked.

"It's a small town, Mr. Daniels. Everyone from Oroville to here has heard of you by now."

Great.

"As you are not officially Mr. Daniels' lawyer, I'm going to have to ask you to leave."

"Actually, Sheriff, I've decided to accept any assistance Mr. Probst is willing to offer," I said. Praswá gawked at me as if I'd lost my mind and started clucking. I needed access to the logging operation, and this seemed the most efficient way in.

"Glad to hear it." Probst placed a hand on my shoulder. "Unless you are prepared to charge my client with something, I think we'll be going as you suggested."

Praswá clenched his jaw but said nothing.

As I got up, I asked, "Can I get my gun back?"

Praswá glared at me. "No, it's evidence in an ongoing investigation."

I looked to Probst. He asked, "Do you have a warrant, Sheriff?"

"No, he volunteered it."

Probst shrugged. "It'll take some time to force its return. I'll do what I can. For now, I am to bring you to Mr. Olesk."

Feeling vulnerable, I had to leave the revolver behind. Outside, a driver stood beside a glimmering Rolls Royce. He opened the door for Probst, who stood aside and motioned for me to get in. Though Praswá had mentioned financial difficulties plaguing those who worked for the logging company, the owner's pockets appeared to remain well-lined.

Radiant Futures Logging Site

Probst directed the driver north.

"Could I trouble you to make a quick stop at my hotel? I'd like to clean myself up. The sheriff banged on my door pretty early."

Probst glanced up as if startled by my presence and disheveled condition. "Oh, yes. Of course. Just tell the driver where to go."

"The Whitestone Hotel, please."

The driver nodded in reply.

Once there, Probst opted to remain with the car. The driver opened my door and proceeded to wipe the accumulated road dust off the Rolls. I shook my head and made for my room. I found Leslie sitting at the desk, studying her books.

"Have fun?" she asked.

"Barrels. The owner of the local logging operation sent his lawyer to get me free. I'm off to see him now. Sheriff Praswá is holding onto my gun for the time being."

Leslie winced. She knew how much I loved both my car and my gun. "I'm sorry, Travis." She brightened. "I found some info about the wolf creatures the elder described to us. They are more commonly known as were-wolves. There's a lot of lore, some of it even suggesting it's a kind of extra-terrestrial parasite spirit. It attaches to a host, gives them the ability to change into humanoid beasts, and feeds off the ensuing carnage."

"Sounds lovely."

"Well, I've also found that it's vulnerable to wolf's bane, but not much else."

"Do we have wolf's bane handy?"

"No. Sorry."

"Figures." I grabbed a clean pair of pants, underwear, soap, and shaving kit and went down the hall to the bathroom. After a quick shower, shave, and change, I returned to the room. "I'm going to need you to poke around town today and see what you can hear concerning the recent vandalism and sabotage. With your ability to avoid notice, you'll hear things most people wouldn't say with others around."

Leslie stared at me dumbfounded.

"What?" I asked.

"You've never let me out on my own, let alone asked me to help snoop."

I shrugged. "You have an advantage we can use to get answers. The faster we figure this out, the faster we can be gone." On my way out, I stopped and pinned her down with a stern look. "Don't do anything to draw attention and be careful."

I knew she rolled her eyes at my back without needing to see it. She didn't see the small smile I allowed to wrinkle the corners of my mouth as I strode down the hall.

The driver was standing beside the Rolls, waiting, when I exited the hotel. The car appeared to have just come off the line, no sign of dust.

Once I was back in the car, we sped off toward the east. The women and children who populated the scattered homes of the residential areas of Tonasket peered out their windows to watch the fancy car roll past. Few left their homes to face the constant clouds of dust and dirt coating everything. It wasn't worth braving the outside for a few moments of sunlight.

We left the town behind, headed into the hills, and entered the vast woodlands dominating the countryside. The lush, green wood vanished as we crossed into the cutting area. Where there once had been a thick, healthy forest of cedar, spruce, and hemlock now stretched a wasteland of destruction. Acres of tree stumps and chewed-up earth surrounded us. It was a shock to drive through a verdant curtain of nature to discover such devastation.

"My god," I whispered.

Probst glanced out the window, used to the horrific view. "Yes, the march of progress is wondrous, is it not? Once we get this sabotage business sorted, we can all go back to work and steer this nation onward to a radiant future."

I could hear the practiced repetition of words handed down by soulless, corporate think tanks. If their idea of the future was a barren world devoid of life, they could keep it. I grew up surrounded by concrete and steel, but I also valued places like Central Park. This harvest of resources without concern for the future sickened me. I kept my face impassive, but I found myself on the side of the vandals if they meant to keep this blight from spreading.

We pulled up to the work site. Massive trees stood as stalwart guardians of the green in the distance. The sound of buzzsaws and axes were absent. Instead, the world was a symphony of hammers and curse words as men struggled to repair damaged machines. Shattered and twisted parts were strewn across the ground between disabled tractors. Saws lay in piles, bent and broken from being used to attack the tractors they were meant to supplement.

Probst led me to a ramshackle building and pushed open the hammered-together wooden door in front of me. Inside, staring at a map of the area, an older man stood over a table made of carpentry horses and plywood. Probst stepped around me and glided over to the older man's side.

"Sir, I've brought the detective."

"Hmm?" The older man, Mr. Olesk, rose to his full height. He was straight-backed, wearing a crisp, white button-down shirt with the sleeves rolled up past his elbows. Sun-tanned skin offset a full head of silver hair. His face appeared carved from the same wood he cut down and sawed into planks to ship across the country to wherever American developers chose to expand next without thought or need. His eyes refocused onto both me and his lawyer, setting aside visions of money and power.

"Oh! Yes, Mr. Daniels, correct? Good of you to come out. We seem to be having a problem."

"I heard. Not sure what else I can provide with the local police already investigating."

"The police?" His lips curled like he'd bit into a rotting apple. "You mean the damned Injun with a badge? It's his kind who are destroying our equipment. He'd sooner let me go bankrupt and all those hard-working men outside, and their families, go hungry for lack of wages than betray his dirt-loving clan."

"I believe they are called a tribe, sir."

"Same thing." Olesk waved away the correction as nothing more than a pointless detail. "The situation cannot go on, and when I heard there was a big-city detective in town, I knew you were sent by God Almighty to bring progress and industry back to these hills."

"I don't know about that, Mr. Olesk."

"The blessed never do, my good man, the blessed never do. I am willing to pay you a great deal of money if you can discover the culprits, and there's even a bonus if you can provide evidence the sheriff is in on it." Olesk flashed a wink at the end.

"I can look into the matter for you, Mr. Olesk. Whatever I find will be turned over to the appropriate parties."

"Wonderful! Probst here will provide you with an advance to get you started."

That bit of business concluded, Olesk's attention turned back to the map, as good as dismissing me.

"One question, before I go." Olesk scowled at me, appearing annoyed to be disturbed after he had already acquired my assistance. "Couldn't your problems be a result of bears or moose or whatever is in the woods? Why are you so certain it's the local tribes?"

"Why?" he roared as if I'd called him a liar. "Come with me!"

He stormed out of the building, clearly expecting me to follow close behind without hesitation. The lawyer offered a weak smile and nodded for me to go first. The logging baron was a virile man regardless of his obvious age and cleared a good distance before I was able to join him outside. I rushed after to catch up while Probst took his time ambling through the cluttered, busy worksite.

Olesk stopped and pointed up at a cliff to the north. "There! They have been there since we started work, always on the edge of my plot, watching. They are there before we arrive and remain until the last man leaves. They watch and watch and watch. Those damned savages say they are standing witness to the desecration of the land. Desecration! I am providing the raw materials to a growing nation. They would have us all living in squalor and wearing rags. Those are the culprits, detective! I have hunted in several of the forests north and south of here. Nothing exists large enough or intelligent enough to cause these kinds of problems."

On the cliff, a small group of men and women stood watching, just as he said. I couldn't make out specific features due to the distance. It was disconcerting how they remained still as statues, staring down on the work site.

"Have they said anything to you? Threatened your operation in any way?"

"They may be savages, sir, but they are not stupid. No. Ever since I tied up their lawsuit against us, they are required to have no direct interaction with me or those under my employ. That cliff marks the very edge of my allotment. In the meantime, while the suit winds its way through the court system, I need to squeeze every ounce of lumber out of this forest just in case I lose, which I'm told is doubtful."

Probst offered a silent nod.

Olesk waved to beckon someone closer. "If you have any more questions, please direct them to Mr. Probst or my site manager, Mr. Williams." Olesk stomped back toward his makeshift office.

"I shall leave you to your work while I search for a way to salvage my own."

I glanced to Probst. "I'd like to know how a man of his age maintains that kind of vitality." He offered a soft chuckle as his only answer.

Williams limped toward us. His face was covered in grease and dirt. He wore similar overalls and work boots to the rest of the crew. As he came closer, I noticed he had only one arm. In fact, as I began to take in my surroundings and noted the men who worked the site, I found that most of those working as temporary mechanics were maimed in some fashion. Those who were guiding the work of others seemed whole, but those who struggled with the work appeared to be missing fingers, hands, feet, arms, legs, and, in two cases I could see, ears.

"What's going on?" Williams interrupted my thoughts. "Why'd the boss wave me over and leave?" He ran grease covered hands down his overalls to clean them. Ignoring me and speaking to Probst, he reached inside one of many side pockets and withdrew a toothpick to chew on.

"Mr. Olesk just hired this man to look into the acts of sabotage and vandalism we've been suffering. You are to give him everything and anything he needs to conclude his business." Probst bowed to me. "When you're finished, I'll meet you with the down payment and have our driver return you to town." With that, he stepped away, following the same path Olesk had taken back to the office building.

I gave Williams an appraising once over and said, "Olesk is convinced your problems are rooted in the local tribes."

"Not the tribes. Just those fools on the cliff. Most of the main tribes have fallen in line and stay silent about the logging. They know we have federal backing. They stay quiet so the government doesn't decide to take more of their reservation and sell it off."

"More? You mean this used to be reservation land?"

"Yeah, all the way up to the Canadian border. When the need for lumber grew, the feds took the northern half and sold off claims and let the tribes keep the southern, less useful half." A perverse grin slid into place like he was sharing a joke with a fellow working stiff.

"Lucky for Mr. Olesk, it seems."

"Lucky for us all. Without the logging industry, most of us would be out of work. This operation provides jobs and local businesses with the cashflow necessary to keep our families and towns alive. The tribes weren't doing anything useful with it. Hunting on occasion, maybe, but they resisted every offer made to harvest the trees here."

"What happened to your arm?"

He considered the empty space his left arm once occupied. "Logging accident. These things happen."

"I can see that."

"Excluding the local farmers who can help with the equipment and guide our guys with the repairs, it would be harder to find a man without injury in this industry. It's better than mining coal a mile underground or inside a mountain. We may lose a limb, but more often than not, we walk away. No danger of cave-ins trapping us in the ground and being buried alive. When we retire, there's no threat of black lung or some other horrible disease that'll cut our lives short once we put the axe down. Logging is tough, but there are worse honest jobs."

"Fair enough. It's kind of Olesk to keep men employed who can't chop wood anymore."

Williams tensed up, insulted. "Kindness has got nothing to do with it. We're still able to drive the tractors and supervise the rookies. We can keep an eye out and make sure no one repeats our mistakes. Olesk is a great boss and a great man. He found me a position in his crew after my accident, but he expects his people to work. Right now, most of the loggers are sitting at home, wasting away beside their families because there's only so much mechanic work to go around. Those of us here just happen to have more experience with the machines or are farmers from around the area."

He was getting heated, which was the point. People slip up when angry. "You say it's the group on the cliff that's harassing the operation. You have any proof?"

Williams took a deep breath to calm himself. He was a smart one. Olesk picked a good man to run his crews. "No evidence as such. But they're always here, and they're the most vocal about how we're hurting the land and endangering everyone by cutting down the forest."

"Endangering how?"

"I don't know. Something about threatening the balance of all life or some superstitious nonsense. One of them even attacked me a few weeks back at a bar because he recognized me from here. They aren't rational, none of them."

"Mind if I take a look at some of the damage?"

We strode to the nearest disabled tractor that men were cannibalizing to repair other nearby machines. It was obvious why some tractors were outright abandoned after seeing twisted frames too damaged to fix in the field.

"And this was done in one night?" I asked.

"Whatever we fix is wrecked by morning."

There was no way a human, or even a dedicated group of humans, could do this kind of damage in a single night. At the same time, what was I going to say? This is the work of were-wolves and sasquatches?

Not likely.

I examined the sight in detail, seeing more and more evidence of supernatural interference. Injured or otherwise, there was an army of men who could stand guard at night and try to catch the perpetrators in action, so why hadn't they done that? Maybe it's a blessing they hadn't. "Haven't you set guards at night to try and catch those responsible?"

"We have. Mr. Olesk won't pay for many of us to stay after. He thinks it's a waste of money that he wouldn't need to pay if the sheriff did his job. Still, he's given in and now is paying for a few men to stay on at night and keep an eye out. It hasn't helped. When they hear something happening, they rush over to check it out. By the time anyone arrives, they're too late and hear something else getting busted up on the other side of the site. We've even tried parking the vehicles close together. Somehow, they keep finding ways of doing enormous amounts of damage in seconds."

"How would one get up on that cliff?"

Williams pointed to a path that dipped out of sight. "There. That path will lead you down and around the base of the cliff and then up. They won't talk to you. They don't talk to anyone outside of their group here or in town, not even their own kind."

"I'm pretty persuasive."

Tonasket, Washington

Leslie explored the downtown area of Tonasket in relative solitude. Not only was the cloaking spell keeping people's attention directed away from her, but most residents were too preoccupied by their own worries to notice the new young woman in town wearing a light-colored blouse and pleated skirt. Men sat in chairs or paced in front of stores, chain-smoking cigarettes while the women about town were minding children or out-of-work husbands.

For the first time since Arkham, Leslie felt free to roam the world again. She regretted that her first taste of freedom was being spent in a town lacking interesting places to visit. Regardless, she had a job to do. The restaurant next to the hotel was empty, so she wandered south where most of the local businesses were. She'd only seen them for an instant when they followed the man on the horse out of town, but it was a place to start.

Along Whitcomb, she passed small offices, a butcher's, a hardware store, and to her delight, Liberty Theatre, a theatre showing talkies. She hoped there would be a chance for her and Travis to sit for a moment and let their cares melt away while watching the wonders of the silver screen. For now, it was unlikely she'd find anyone inside talking while the shows played. She kept walking and turned right onto Fourth toward a cluster of buildings. There was a bustle of activity passing through the intersection ahead, and she rushed onward to catch up.

She came to the end of the block and turned the corner at Cloud-Dodge General Store where she'd seen the crowd heading and found desperate souls looking for work. Some ambled outside the general store while others knocked on the doors of small offices along the main drive. The largest group had clustered in front of the auto parts store and attached repair garage. A man was waving people away as she slipped closer to listen in.

"I got no work for any of you. I'm sorry."

"Come on, Jack! Anything. We're starving here."

"You and everybody else, Walt. I can't pay you for work I don't have."

The men stalked away, grumbling about skinflints and heartless men.

"At least he acknowledged us," one of the men said.

"Yeah, only because he lives here and isn't holed up in one of these offices where he can ignore us. I don't got hard feelings toward Jack, though. He would give us work if he had it. But Radiant Futures and the Great Northeastern should be helping us out. We break our backs for those companies and get paid pennies while they rake in the profit. Look at him over there!" The man nodded toward a well-dressed man eating on the veranda of a near-empty restaurant. "Living it up while the rest of us watch our families starve. They're punishing us for what those Indians are doing."

"You don't know it's them," replied one of the younger men.

"Of course we do! If it had been one of us, the sheriff would have us in jail already. It's only because it's his own people messing things up that he doesn't arrest them. Should have never given the reservation the right to vote."

The conversation continued down the street, but Leslie had already split off to from the group to eavesdrop on the well-dressed man. As she moved into a position to hear better, she discovered another gentleman in a cheap, wrinkled suit hidden behind a decorative plant, and sitting across from the first. The second man ate nothing, busy mopping sweat from his brow.

"Sir," the sweaty man said, "I understand your position, but Mr. Olesk is doing everything he can to mitigate the damage and keep production—"

"Councilman Davers, I appreciate Radiant Futures' efforts, but effort does not fill transport cars on our railway. If they cannot provide enough lumber to stock the local stores and support local expansion, how can I justify the expense to keep cars sitting in my yards when I could move them to more industrious locations?"

"Mr. Crest, the towns along your line depend on the rail system for transportation to jobs, doctor's appointments, and visiting family. We can't afford you to cease operations."

"You have nothing to worry about there, sir. We would never think of ending our residential service."

Davers sighed. "Good. Good. The rest of the council will be heartened to know we can still rely on continued service. I hope this extends to outside goods coming in as well."

Crest nodded as he used his knife and fork to cut away dime-sized portion of egg salad sandwich. "Of course, however, the cost will need to increase." He swallowed the small bite and took a drink of water which held a thin slice of lemon floating on top. "In deference to your town's need and unfortunate circumstances, I would be willing to increase the shipping costs a mere fifty percent."

"What?"

"Spread out across Oroville down to Okanogan, of course. I'll leave the specifics to your various mayors, councils, departments, and shop owners. Since we will not have outgoing resources to cover our operating costs when we leave town with empty cars, your towns will be expected to offset our losses."

"Now wait a second, empty cars are light and with a decrease in operations, you'll have a decrease in necessary manpower and fuel. Half of your full operating costs is the same as paying full price. We can't afford—"

"Yes, all good points, councilman. I see how you were elected. We can come down to thirty-seven percent of the original costs. This is our final offer."

Councilman Davers sputtered, at a loss for words, but only a brief fit before asking, "And if we can solve this issue and resume logging operations?"

"Well, then, we can forget this whole conversation and move on as we always have. Though, I find it better to be clear about all possibilities so no one is caught unaware. In the eyes of Great Northeastern, the trains will run as long as someone has paid for a ticket."

Crest didn't seem to care either way about the sabotage, though he was happy to take advantage of the situation. He patted his mouth with a cloth napkin, set it beside the unfinished meal, and stood to leave. Crest was gone by the time Davers realized he'd been left with the bill. "Scoundrel!" Davers slapped some money on the table and stormed out.

Leslie decided to follow Councilman Davers, as he seemed the most invested of the two parties in the current crisis. He walked to Western Ave and turned south. Davers grumbled to himself the whole way but remembered to wave and smile to everyone and every business owner he passed. The hollow quiet of Turpin and Eaton Garage felt unnatural as they passed. Men dressed in overalls stood around tinkering with the parts laying around. Deep-set eyes tracked Davers as he passed. Jack's garage wasn't the only one suffering a lack of work.

A little farther up, Davers stepped into a large, red building with the word "LUMBER" painted along the side. The smell of sawdust hung in the air like the ghost of lost prosperity. Davers entered the massive building, his steps echoing off the walls. To the left stood a small office built into the front corner of the warehouse. Davers threw open its door and stepped in. Leslie sidled up to the wall and tried to listen.

"Woodbury, we need to do something about the Radiant Futures problem."

"Way to state the obvious, Pete."

"I just got done talking to the Northeastern rep. They want to charge us an additional thirty-seven percent shipping to bring supplies into town if we can't get the exports going again."

"Jesus. The logging issues are killing me, but that'll kill the whole town."

"Not just us. Every town up and down the line."

"Greedy bastards."

"We need to pressure the sheriff to start getting answers. You know the local marshal; can you get him to look into it?"

"I already tried. He said it's not federal. Maybe if we can prove the tribes living on the reservation are involved, he might be able to act, but the ones Olesk keeps accusing all live in the towns. They cut ties with the reservation."

"Great. God-damned savage sheriff isn't going to do shit."

"We could talk to some of the mayors of the other towns. Maybe they could put some extra pressure on the sheriff to move faster."

"Or we can get the townspeople involved."

"Is that smart? It could get out of hand."

"Who cares? We need this dealt with. I won't have this town, along with all the others, be destroyed because of a bunch of thugs who value trees more than people."

"I guess, but we need to be careful."

Leslie slunk away from the door and exited the warehouse. The men carried on their plans to rouse the locals up and down the railway. They were all dependent on the logging business in some fashion. With people's livelihoods on the line, nothing good would come of manufacturing outrage. She made her way back toward the hotel. She needed to think about their options, maybe find something in her books.

If this only concerned humans, it was guaranteed to get ugly. Knowing the were-wolves and sasquatch waited in the darkness, ready to lash out at anyone who threatened to violate the forest, it promised to become bloody. Leslie felt tears burning her eyes. She wasn't sure if it was sadness, frustration, or both.

həⱡn̓cicň' i? t c̓lc̓al'

The trail up to the top of the cliff was well tread. Dress shoes weren't designed for crushed gravel, but I made my way without slipping too much. The group of men and women watching the logging crew fix the machines turned their heads just enough to find me coming around the final, rocky corner. Deciding I represented nothing important, they returned to their mission of bearing witness to the devastation of the sacred forest.

"I need to speak with whoever leads this group."

No one made an effort to reply. They remained as silent as the statues of kings or guards overlooking a realm in which they no longer held sway. I approached with slow, deliberate steps. I didn't want to give them the impression I was hostile. I also didn't want to slip and tumble down the cliff face.

"I understand there's some tensions between you, your tribe, and the logging operations."

Still, they remained silent.

I had one more card to play, but I didn't like exposing how much I knew this early. However, I needed answers. "I witnessed a child being attacked and killed by a large wolf up in the Monashee Mountains. Any of you have something to do with that?"

The attention of the group snapped to me in an instant. The united movement set me off balance. One woman broke from the group and stalked toward me, while the others returned to watch the loggers. The fierceness in her eyes held me in place. Well-muscled and features as hard as stone… on any other occasion I would have been in love enough to ask her out for a drink just to stare into those cobalt eyes.

"What did you see?" She was in her mid-thirties with long black hair, rugged clothes, and a small, metal amulet around her neck. The amulet looked like a hand-crafted wolf's head. "What do you know?"

Hands held up, palms out, I said, "Just what I saw and what your elder told me. I just want to figure out what attacked the child and stop any trouble that may arise from misunderstandings all around."

The woman simmered with rage. "The elders have abandoned the land. We have not. We don't answer to the tribe any longer."

"I honestly don't care about any of that," I said. "My name is Travis Daniels. I'm just looking into the matter for your elder, and into the sabotage for Mr. Olesk. I have no opinions regarding the situation, and I only really care about the murder. I just want to make sure no innocent people are hurt. What's your name?"

She scowled at me for a moment before replying, "You can call me Ntlʕánaʔ."[1]

"Fair enough, Ntlʕánaʔ. Were any of your people in the mountains two days ago?"

---

1. Pack Leader. Pronounced: en·tl·Ä·nā.

"No. None of us would ever venture there. It is not our place. It is theirs."

"Whose?"

Ntlʕánaʔ didn't answer.

"Your elder—"

"He is no longer our elder. We broke away from the main tribe when they chose to bow to your invader government. Our people lost much when the white men came. We were given a corner of our own lands as a gift." Ntlʕánaʔ scoffed. "Imagine being gifted what cannot be owned. Then, to have that gift carved up and sold when it's decided the resources are too valuable to leave in the hands of 'ignorant savages'."

I didn't know what to say. She wasn't wrong, but it also wasn't the reason I was there.

"There was a murder in Monashee. A child was being attacked by a very large wolf. I shot it. The bullets bounced off. It ran when... something called to it, or maybe it heard someone bigger coming."

Fear widened Ntlʕánaʔ's eyes for less than a second before her emotionless mask fell back into place. She called over her people and asked them something in their native language. It was too much and too fast to track. She turned back and shook her head. "None of us were in Monashee. You are wrong about what you saw."

"I'm not. Forest rangers and the local sheriff tracked down the place I fired my weapon. They found the bullets, gouge marks in the trees, and a lot of blood. They know something happened out there, and it's got the authorities and Elder Chelahitsa worried."

By now, the rest of the group were listening. All of them began arguing in a low murmur, throwing suspicious glances my way. The word sc̓xʷanʕáy̓tm̓ was thrown around often. When N̓tlʕánaʔ noticed me focusing on what they were saying, she hushed everyone. "Did you see them?"

I nodded. Admitting what I'd seen in words was still too much. Even after everything in Arkham, to acknowledge any of it tilted the scales of reality.

"Did they see the attacker?"

I tried to recall the night, the timing, everything. It was all too blurry, hidden behind a filmy curtain of the worry I harbored for Leslie at the time. "I don't know. But the marks of the child's body were deep and obvious."

"cx̌aʔx̌áʔ sc̓xʷxtwixʷ!"[2] cried out one of the group.

N̓tlʕánaʔ hushed him.

"What does that mean?"

They stared at me and turned away to resume their vigil over the logging site. "Tell Elder Chelahitsa to cower on his ranch as these men destroy our lands. Tell the sheriff to kowtow to his bureaucratic masters. This is not their concern. Do not return here." N̓tlʕánaʔ turned away and joined the others.

"Are you the ones vandalizing the equipment?"

They ignored me.

"Is something, or someone else destroying it?"

Nothing.

---

2. Sacred Agreement. Pronounced: chä·HA- sch·hoo·TWEE·hoo.

"Fine. Don't talk to me, but whatever is going on out here, it's going to turn worse if the vandalism continues. You're threatening people's livelihoods, their families. These towns need the work. I've seen what mobs can turn into. This will only get worse until someone is killed."

They stared out over the remains of the forest. Nothing I said made any one of them waver in their commitment to bear witness. I hoped they weren't the ones coming down at night and wrecking the equipment. Olesk considered them guilty, and if enough workers decided the same, the rest of the town would soon follow. I didn't want to see anyone get hurt, but I knew with the storms brewing on the horizon in every direction, this wasn't going to end without a lot of pain.

I retraced the path back down to the site and found Probst standing nearby holding an envelope. Williams had joined a group of three men examining a tractor, pondering the best methods of repair. Probst offered the envelope to me. "This should get you started. If you require more in your efforts, please contact me. My card is within."

Inside the envelope was a check made out to me for one hundred dollars. "No offense, counselor, but I'm not big on checks and especially ones from a hurting business."

Probst stiffened, but the wooden facsimile of a smile never flickered. "I assure you, Mr. Daniels, the check will clear the bank. There is one just down the street from where you are staying. If you have any problem, just call." Probst withdrew a slim money clip and peeled away a twenty-dollar bill. "Will this assuage your worries?"

I took the bill and stuffed it into my pocket. The envelope disappeared into my jacket. "No problem. Mind giving me a ride back to my hotel?"

"Of course, just this way."

The car, shining and devoid of dust, was turned around and waiting.

Whitestone Diner

As I entered the room, Leslie jumped out of the desk chair, soaring over her array of ancient tomes, and rushed up to me. "We need to figure this out fast," she said. "The town council is going to rally the people against the tribes and blame them for the problems at the logging site."

I shrugged off my coat and tossed it onto the back of the desk chair. "They won't have much difficulty with that. All the workers at the site already think it's the Colville tribes, specifically the Okanogans, or at least the ones watching them day and night. After what I saw, they may be right."

"What?"

"Well, in part, at least. The damage showed evidence of extraordinary strength, deep gashes, and twisted parts. It could be the warrior were-wolves, the sasquatch, or both. I'm betting on both, to be honest."

"Can you blame them?" Leslie sat on the edge of her bed. "They had so much taken from them." Leslie went rigid with surprise. "You don't think they're responsible for the attack on the mountain, too, do you?"

"They may be guilty of the sabotage, but I don't suspect they had anything to do with that. When I mentioned it, they were all shocked by the news. Their leader, a fierce woman—you'd like her—didn't strike me as easily rattled. She didn't know what to make of what we saw. Which begs the question, if it wasn't the tribal were-wolves, then who was it? Chelahitsa didn't mention anything about other were-wolves in the area." I searched the room for food of any kind as I talked, forgetting for a moment we didn't live in a rented apartment anymore. "Come on. We should grab a bite. There's a cafe next door."

Leslie nodded and followed me down. "You said the town council is getting involved somehow?" I asked. She recounted the conversation between the railroad representative and the councilman followed by the one Davers had with the local businessman. "That's all we need," I said. "Panicked towns and mob justice. This is building faster than I thought it would."

Across from the hotel, in the open field, people started gathering as the sun dipped below the horizon. Everyone milled about, saying hello to neighbors and whispering to each other. We entered the cafe and found some seats by the window. I wanted to keep an eye on any event that could further the complications multiplying around us.

The diner was well-kept, glossy white and shining metal. A man stood behind a counter reading the local newspaper. The headline, "VANDALISM, SABOTAGE HALTS LOGGING!" filled the space above the fold. The local economic repercussions took up the rest of the front-page. With everything Leslie overheard, there was a lot of money being disrupted in the towns north and south of the logging site. A murder in the woods was bad, but money will get a lot more innocent people killed while the real criminals get richer.

We ordered a couple of tuna sandwiches, coffee for me, and tea for Leslie. When our food came out, Leslie tapped my hand and pointed. "That's him! Councilman Davers."

A red-faced man with a too-eager smile waded through the mob, shaking any free, empty hand within reach. Sheriff Praswá followed close behind. He nodded to a handful of people in the crowd and ignored the unkind stares stabbed in his direction. Davers stood up on a sturdy crate placed at the head of the crowd and patted the air for silence. The owner of the cafe stepped out from behind the counter and stood with the door open to listen. Davers's words drifted to us through the bitter night.

"Everyone, I know you are all concerned about the situation with Radiant Futures and the problems they're having. I asked our mutual friends and neighbors to spread the word about tonight so the sheriff and I could assure you all we are doing everything we can to identify the vandals and get you all back to work."

A man shouted from within the crowd, "What if the problem is with the tribe? Will the sheriff side with the law or his own kind?"

Praswá stepped forward to confront the crowd. "Whoever breaks the laws I was elected to uphold, regardless of who they are or where they live, will be arrested and prosecuted."

"Even the people who got you elected?"

"As far as I'm concerned, I was elected by the people, and I work for the people. I don't care who you voted for."

The crowd grumbled but didn't pursue the issue under Praswá's stony glare. Davers cleared his throat, towering over the crowd atop his crate. "My friends, I have spoken with not only our town council, but also members of other town councils and mayors north and south of us along the rail line. We are all united, resolved to overcome this obstacle to our future prosperity."

Another man yelled from the side. "That's all well and good, but what about our missing cattle? The loggers aren't the only people who live here, Councilman!"

"We've been looking into that, sir," began Praswá, "and we suspect it to be the actions of wild animals, possibly rabid. We ask all farmers and herdsmen to remain indoors at night. I've contacted forest rangers and other services to hunt down the animals raiding your pens. Do not try and deal with it yourself."

"Well, it sounds as if our sheriff is on the job. Thank you for coming out—"

"Good man, there," said the proprietor as he allowed the door to swing closed. "A true civil servant. That sheriff could learn a lot from Mr. Davers. The sooner we clear these damned Indians out of our towns and down to their reservation where they belong, the better."

Leslie leaned forward, ready to argue, but I placed my hand over hers and shook my head. "It's not worth it," I whispered. "Focus on the case. Prove they're innocent and the rest will attend to itself. We need people to cooperate with us if we're going to get answers."

She leaned back, her jaw clenching with the frustration of righteous youth. I remembered that kind of drive when starting out as a rookie policeman. The realities of the job wore it down faster than anyone expected. I couldn't decide if I envied Leslie just then or mourned for the day the world would grind that defiance to dust.

For now, it was enough to see it blazing across the table, ready to burn through the darkness of human nature.

We finished our meal and returned to the room. While Leslie got ready for bed in the hallway bathroom, my fingers itched to check over my gun, to clean and oil it. Would the Radiant Futures lawyer, Probst, even bother to force the sheriff to return it? When the greatest dangers to my life, at the moment, were primeval giants and were-creatures impervious to bullets, losing the gun for a short period shouldn't have been my biggest concern.

But I'd seen what happened when mobs started looking for someone to blame. Weapons of every stripe appear in idle hands, and fear turns everything into a viable target.

Murder Scene

A rapid knocking at the door sent streaks of red into the peaceful darkness of sleep. I didn't bother with putting on a dress shirt before yanking the door open. It was like this town had something against letting anyone sleep in. Praswá stood there with deep bags under his eyes. It appeared he'd gotten less sleep than me. My holster and gun hung from his shoulder. Without a word, he offered it back.

I took it and waited.

"The bullets you fired came back clean. Seems you missed whatever you shot at."

I tilted my head back and to the side, inviting him in. Once I hung the holster on the chair, I began searching for a clean shirt.

Praswá continued speaking. "There was an attack at the logging site. Three dead. Mr. Olesk and his attorney are demanding your involvement. To be honest, I may need it as well."

I glanced at my gun. "You and I both know that isn't going to do much."

"The gun isn't for that."

"Last night's 'town meeting'?"

Praswá sighed and shook his head. "I told him it was a bad idea."

"Mind giving me a few minutes to clean up?"

"Yeah, I'll meet you downstairs in the lobby."

He closed the door on his way out. I turned to Leslie asleep in her bed and delivered a sharp kick to the frame to shake her awake. "Three people are dead at the logging site. We're heading out there with the sheriff. I'm hitting the shower."

Leslie groaned. "Oh, how I've missed your gentle way of waking me up. We need to find a place with two rooms again."

With a small bundle of clothes under my arm, I retreated to the shower. The idea of finding the stability necessary to build a home again seemed unlikely. Saying any of that to Leslie felt like cruelty. A quick shower and shave later, Leslie and I met Praswá downstairs.

"About time, Daniels. Not as if people's lives are at stake."

"Sheriff, I'd like to introduce you to my colleague, Leslie Owens." Praswá blinked as if a mist cleared from his vision. Confusion twisted his features as he tried to understand why he only just noticed the young woman to my side.

"Apologies, miss. I'm tired and a little out of it. I'm not sure this is something..."

"It's ok, sheriff. I've seen some things working with Travis."

Praswá shook his head in sadness. "A hard vocation for someone so young to take up. I hope you find a better path in the future." Praswá looked at me. "No offense."

I smiled. "Couldn't agree with you more, sheriff."

We piled into the sheriff's car and made the long drive out to the logging site. "I'm surprised you left to come get me."

"I left some deputies behind to guard and note the scene. But I also wanted to talk to you on the way. To clear the air, as it were."

"Figured."

"I'm calling it an animal attack."

I barked a laugh. "Not a lie, per se."

"This is serious, Daniels. A lot of townsfolk think crazy things about the tribes. My job is to keep the peace. I won't feed their racism."

"Crazier than the truth?"

"You'd be surprised."

I thought it over. "A year ago, maybe. Now, I'm hard to surprise. But I'll admit my encounter in the woods was unexpected."

"You willing to tell me all of it now?"

"Big wolf, small hairy child, pissed giant, hairy parents. What more do you need to know?"

"Anything unusual about the big wolf?"

I coughed from laughing so hard.

Praswá chuckled along. "Stupid question."

Leslie gasped as we broke through the curtain of cedar, spruce, and hemlock trees. Praswá jolted at the sound before searching the car to find Leslie. He shook off the sensation of surprise and mumbled, "I need to sleep." I wanted to tell him it wasn't his fault, but trying to add more supernatural shenanigans to the situation didn't seem useful.

We pulled up to the site and found a crowd of workers surrounding the makeshift office building Olesk used. Deputies stood around the crime scene taking notes. Probst approached the car as soon as we stopped.

"Thank you for retrieving our investigator, sheriff."

"Of course, counselor." Praswá marched toward his scene, leaving us behind with the lawyer.

"I hope you didn't encounter any problem cashing the check, Mr. Daniels?"

"Haven't had a chance yet. The sheriff was at my door bright and early. Considering what he told me, I'm not surprised by the need for urgency."

"Yes, quite the tragedy. We've never had problems with animal attacks in the past. I fear it's a result of the added patrols we implemented at night to prevent vandalism. Mr. Olesk is beside himself."

"With grief or rage?"

Probst blinked with manufactured innocence. "I would think either or both would be an appropriate response."

He wasn't wrong. I motioned for Leslie to make her way over to the makeshift office while I joined Praswá by the bodies. Ragged slashes had torn through clothes and skin, broken bones, and severed joints.

"You moved the bodies?"

Praswá nodded. "Yeah, but I marked where we found each piece. Parts were everywhere and I wanted to make sure we had everything."

I flashed a silent question, but he waved it off for later. It was strange how fast I fell back into the police officer shorthand when in the presence of friendly law enforcement.

About twenty yards away, the markers lay scattered over the work area. Whatever attacked made a mess of the poor souls who were only guilty of protecting their livelihood. I walked the scene alongside Praswá, checking the spread of the markers. The deputies had color coded each one to identify which victim's body part landed where. It was a tangled mess.

"This isn't going to end well."

Praswá grunted.

"What are you standing around staring at?" Olesk exploded out of his shed-like office and stomped across the crime scene, ignoring anyone who tried to stop him "You know who did this! Go arrest them!" He pointed at the clifftop. The empty ledge seemed incomplete without its silent witnesses.

"Mr. Olesk, we are still gathering evidence. For all appearances, this was a tragic animal attack—"

"Don't give me that! I know how you people can influence animals and make it look like wildlife passed by. I won't be fooled by your tricks! Now do your damn job! Arrest those people who've been looming over my operation, or my men will do it for you."

I waited for the tough guy response from Praswá, but it never came. He ignored the old man's bluster and continued to examine the scene.

"Do you hear me?"

Praswá turned to me. "Seen enough?"

"For now. They show all the signs of an animal attack, but that doesn't rule out an animal being driven here by a more human suspect. We should at least question the ones who were up there. From what I've learned, they are always here. So why not today?"

"Exactly!" bellowed Olesk. "Finally, a real law man to speak sense!"

"Fair point, Mr. Daniels." Praswá lead the way back to where they'd arranged the body parts without bothering to glance at Olesk. I was starting to really like the sheriff. Somehow, I managed to suppress my smile. Olesk grumbled something and stomped back to his shed. A quick nod to Leslie had her moving to find the best position to listen in on him from outside.

"You know all those stories of native magic to drive animals is nonsense, right?"

"Of course, but it got Olesk off your back and gave us a reason to talk with the həłn'cičn'."

"Nice pronunciation. N'səl'xčin'[1] isn't an easy language to pick up."

"Dumb luck."

"We should stay out of their way."

"Not an option and you know it. If we don't shut this down, it'll boil over into a war. A lot of innocent people on both sides will get hurt. I didn't want to get involved, but now that I am, I can't let that happen."

"Why did you get involved?"

A quick glance at Leslie brought Praswá's attention to her again. "Ah, I see."

We stood over the mangled corpses of three large, muscular men who'd been torn apart. Blood soaked the ground, transforming it into black mud. Deep gashes cut across what was left of their torsos. A blind man could tell they were claw marks. I leaned to

---

1. Syilx Language. Pronounced: en·selhk·CHEEN.

speak into the sheriff's ear. "Are we sure this isn't the others from up north?"

He nodded. "Definitely big wolves."

A bit of movement brought my attention up to meet the eyes of Mr. Williams, the site foreman. He glared down on the three bodies with a barely contained outrage. A tug at Praswá's sleeve stole his attention from the scene so I could redirect it onto Williams.

"Charles, I assume you assigned these men to guard duty last night?"

"Yeah, they needed the extra cash." A tear slipped down one cheek. I felt for the guy. He'd sent these men to their deaths and had no way of knowing what horrors they encountered before the end.

"Sorry for your loss, Williams," I said, "but you need to know this isn't your fault. You couldn't have known a wild animal was going to happen onto the site."

Williams stared through me like I was a ghost haunting his nightmare, unsure of why I came or bothered to speak. He refocused after a long pause and nodded. "I know it's not my fault, Mr. Daniels." He shot a look at Praswá. "Excuse me, but I need to head into town and notify their families."

Praswá stood up. "I think you should let me handle that, Charles."

"You do what you want. But these men were working under my watch, and I'll talk to whomever I wish."

The two men stared at each other before Williams was summoned by Mr. Olesk to the office shack. Williams strode across the ground ready to stomp over anyone or thing that had the misfortune to be in his way. Leslie watched him enter the shack and continued to listen.

"That one is going to stir up trouble," I said.

"If it wasn't him, it would be someone else." Praswá rubbed at his eyes. "I'll go find Michele and talk to her about this."

"Michele?"

"She's the leader of the rogue həłn'cičn'."

"Good luck. I met her yesterday and she is a woman of few begrudging words."

A small truck pulled up and a pale-faced man got out and rushed over to the scene carrying a small medical bag in one hand and what appeared to be white sheets under his other arm.

"Who's this guy?"

"Our local mortician. He'll gather the bodies and transport them back to town." Praswá met the grub-skinned man and helped carry the sheets over to the bodies. I moved out of their way and let them get to work covering the bodies. Once the deputies were set to their tasks, Praswá directed me back to his car.

I waved Leslie over but intercepted her halfway between. "Learn anything?"

"Nothing but a whole lot of superstitions and ranting."

"Anything credible?"

"I'll check my books when I get back, but I doubt it. Sounded like he was making it up as he went along."

Praswá stared at me. "What are you doing? We need to move on this before it spirals out of control."

The three dismembered corpses being collected for transport trumpeted the imminent arrival of chaos and sorrow. We'd lost control a long time ago.

Meeting Grounds

"You mind dropping us at the Elder's ranch? I want to update him on what we've found."

Praswá nodded. "Yeah, I may as well head there too and see if he can narrow down my search. The həłn'cicŋ' may have broken away from the tribe, but some would still maintain good relations to their immediate family." His lips broke into a small smile. "You're working for the tribe and Radiant Futures?"

"Why not? They both want to know what's happening. I told both I would report the truth and pass any applicable findings onto the authorities. As long as they pay, I don't much care if they like what gets revealed." Praswá gave me a surprised glance. "Within reason, of course. I'm not trying to end up in a sanitarium."

Memories of the last one I'd stumbled through flared to life. The smell of chemicals, gun powder, and blood took my senses on a detour through time. I shook off the recollections and the odors faded. "I just want to figure out who was in the woods that night and see that the child's parents are given justice."

"You've accepted all this remarkably well."

A sour chuckle rumbled from my throat. "We've seen worse."

"Sounds like a story."

"More like a nightmare and one neither of us wants to tempt returning."

"Fair enough."

The drive proceeded in silence until we turned onto Chelahitsa's ranch. The tall man with the horse leaned against the corner of the main house. He nodded and acknowledged our arrival with a quick flick of his fingers before ambling off deeper into the ranch. Had he been expecting us?

"Who is that? Some kind of bodyguard for Chelahitsa?"

Praswá shook his head. "It's not for me to say." He got out and proceeded toward the house.

"What does that mean?" Leslie asked.

"No idea. A tribal thing, maybe?" We got out of the car and followed Praswá to the door. Chelahitsa waved us in and offered seats at the small table in his kitchen. There were five chairs around the table like he knew we would be coming together. Cups of coffee or tea were set at each place.

"Good to see you, Praswá. Been a while."

"Been busy."

"What can I do for you?"

"I need to find Michele. There was an attack at the logging site. Three men are dead."

"You suspect Michele?"

"I don't know what to think, but I need to follow up on it."

Chelahitsa leaned back in his seat. "I don't know where they are. Last I heard, they were keeping vigil over the logging."

"They didn't show up today."

"I know some of the həłn'cicň' found rooms for rent on the outskirts of Okanogan. You could try there."

I interjected. "I'm sorry, isn't Okanogan the name of your tribe?"

Chelahitsa nodded. "And the name of one of the local towns."

"That's not confusing."

Praswá leaned forward. "I was hoping you could ask around with family members and—"

"No. They may have broken away and ignored the tribal council's chosen path forward, but they are still of the tribe."

"I understand. I had to ask."

"Of course, Praswá. I know you are forced to keep a foot in each world."

Praswá laid a hand on Chelahitsa's shoulder and patted as he stood up from the table. "You need me to wait to take you back to Tonasket?"

Chelahitsa waved Praswá away. "I'll have someone take care of them. They have business to attend to here."

Praswá didn't bother to question Chelahitsa or seek my assent before walking out. Once Chelahitsa had spoken, no further discussion was required.

"So, what have you discovered, Mr. Daniels?"

"Not much. The attack was done by a werewolf. The overall damage at the site may be from the həłn'cicň', but some of the machines up there are pretty big. Unless I've misjudged the strength of həłn'cicň', they aren't strong enough for that. I suspect some of the sasquatch are already south and are assisting in sabotaging the site. Once word travels down to them, a fight is only a matter of time. To add to that, a Mr. Davers or the Tonasket Council as a whole is rallying all the towns up and down the Northeastern rail line against not only the həłn'cicn', but all the tribes of the reservations. I'm not sure Sheriff Praswá will be able to stop what's coming."

Chelahitsa rubbed at his temples, mumbling in N'səɫxcin' to himself. "You have an interesting definition of 'not much'."

"Sorry. I like to offer my client solutions, not more problems."

"An admirable intention and one I may be able to help you facilitate."

Chelahitsa stood up and walked outside. We followed him through the ranch until we arrived at a small garage with two vehicles. A Ford Model AA stood in the shadows, covered in mud and dust, alongside an Oldsmobile F-29. A young man, tall and bulky, was busy wiping down the Oldsmobile but stopped when Chelahitsa entered.

"James, these are the two requested by the sc̓xʷanʕáy̓tm'. You will drive them up to the Monashee Mountains and act as a translator so they may speak with one another."

"Wait a second," I said. "You want me to meet with the same creatures who wanted to kill us a few days ago?"

"Have no fear. They sent word and requested a meeting. They were shocked and enraged. After many messages, we've managed to calm them enough to allow for a discussion, but they require your presence to hear what you have to say. They consider you a neutral party."

"And if they don't like what I have to say?"

"Then the town's intentions will be the least of our worries."

Chelahitsa motioned at James. "He will serve as ambassador and translator. Follow his instructions and you will be safe." Having said all he deemed necessary, Chelahitsa walked back toward his house.

A deep, guttural voice rumbled from James's throat, "We can leave when you are ready."

I risked a glance at Leslie, considering asking her to stay behind, but she had already fixed her eyes on me in warning to not even try. "Ready when you are, boss."

The drive took the better part of the day. Either James or Chelahitsa thought ahead and packed some sandwiches and jars of water for the ride.

In between bites, I asked, "How did you learn the sasquatch language?"

He stared ahead at the road. "My mother taught me."

"I assume her parents taught her?"

"Yes."

The longer I stared at him, I noticed little things: the size of his forehead, the thickness of his hair, the broad, squat features. His enormous hands held the steering wheel like one might clutch an egg on the edge of cracking. Everything he did was gentle. Dark hair peeked out from under his sleeves, creeping up onto the back of his hand. I faced forward, went back to eating my sandwich, and resolved to stay quiet.

When we arrived at the base of Monashee, I went to direct James toward the path we'd taken, but he already seemed to know where to go. He managed to drive closer to the tree line than I would have dared before parking. We continued on foot through the woods until we reached the clearing where we first encountered the werewolf, the child, and the sasquatch.

An altar-like pyre filled the center of the clearing. James motioned for Leslie and me to stand on the side opposite of where the sasquatch emerged on the night of the attack. We stood there in the unnatural silence. I couldn't shake the sense that even the trees mourned the loss of the innocence they'd been forced to confront. Figures stepped into the clearing. The soft rustle of leaves in their wake sounded like a breeze flowing through the bows. Their size defied the careful steps which allowed the hulking behemoths to slip through the foliage. The first sasquatch, a female, melted into view carrying the child's body. She stood, back straight, yet solemn, as the others filtered in to take positions around the edge of their half of the clearing. A final two stepped into view holding torches and remained behind their leader. All the sasquatch deferred to the female carrying the child.

The matriarch stepped forward, placed the child on the pyre, and stepped back. Under the light of day, I could see the matted fur, sharp teeth, and vicious claws of the beings who claimed the mountain as their own. Their features were closer to that of a gorilla, yet they wore their emotions as any human might. After the matriarch bowed to James, all the sasquatch lowered themselves to the ground in practiced unison. Even with Leslie and me standing and the sasquatch sitting, we still had to look up into their bright blue eyes.

James stepped forward and bowed to the child and those gathered across from us. He spoke in guttural tones I could never replicate without risking a very sore throat. The matriarch grunted and rumbled in response.

"She says, 'Welcome, defender. We apologize for our rash actions three nights ago. Thank you for attending.'"

"No need to apologize. I understand your reaction. What happened is a great tragedy."

"We were told by the tribes what you saw, but we wish to hear it directly," their leader replied.

"I came here when I heard a scream and commotion. When I entered, I saw the child being attacked by a werewolf."

The assembly of sasquatch growled at that, some eyeing James with deep suspicion. James ignored the looks and focused on his job as interpreter.

"Yes, the marks on the body match those of the həłn̓cicn̓ iʔ t c̓lc̓aƚ. The elder hired you to search for the truth. Have you found the one responsible?"

"Not yet. When I spoke with the həłn̓cicn̓ iʔ t c̓lc̓aƚ, they appeared both alarmed and concerned by what happened. I am still looking into what occurred here."

The matriarch remained quiet for a long time before grunting. "We will wait one more day before beginning our trek south. It is our opinion that this tragedy is rooted in the destruction of the green. The cx̌aʔx̌áʔ sc̓x̌ʷxtwixʷ holds still, but our patience wavers."

"We'll find whoever did this," Leslie said. Her hands creaked under the strain of the fists she made.

The matriarch grinned and bowed slightly to Leslie. I was shocked at the ease with which they saw through her cloak. Something to remember and consider in the future. I stepped forward to regain their leader's attention. "I'm sorry if this is inappropriate, but may I examine the child's body?"

The other sasquatch grumbled amongst themselves, but a loud huff from the matriarch silenced them. She took a step back and motioned for me to proceed. I stepped up and tried to show as much respect as possible while I checked over the body.

Closer, I saw the deceased child was a young boy. They had washed and brushed his coat. There was no sign of blood or dirt. The slashes were still visible and ragged. I wanted to probe the depth but decided that would be too much for them to suffer. The boy's knuckles and palms were scratched and had mild bruising. Some of the nails were chipped and cracked. He had fought back. Good for him. Without thinking, I laid a hand on his head and smoothed back the hair above his brow. I glanced up, afraid I had erred, but only saw sorrow in their eyes.

I stepped back and bowed to the assembly.

The matriarch stepped forward once again, tears glistening within her fur-covered cheeks. "We will seal our pact in fire and blood."

The torchbearers lumbered forward and placed the torches down on either side of the pyre. As the flames spread, the gathered sasquatch erupted in a chorus of moans, a funeral dirge for their lost loved one. The level of anguish expressed in that wordless—or at least wordless to me—hymn broke over me like a wave. Even after living a life of solitude, shut off and numb to the pain and death of the world, I couldn't steel myself against the power of their shared sorrow. The sharpness of that pain would dull for them through mutual support. It was something I'd never had. That kind of communal support was being abandoned by the whole country in the face of industry and advancement.

A searing ignited in my throat and burned at the corners of my eyes. I pushed it down and excused it as a reaction to the smoke from the pyre. Leslie's throat hitched with a sob, but she stood strong as the flames climbed into the sky. The fire devoured the physical remnants of the cruelty committed against a people who wished to live with nature and be left alone. More would be necessary to quell the emotional toll. I wanted to chastise Leslie for her impetuous promise, but I found myself growling those same words in a silent oath while staring into the crackling flames. Instead, I wrapped my arm around her and pulled her close.

When the fire died down and all that remained were bones, the assembly of sasquatch took turns dropping heaps of dirt onto the glowing coals to snuff them out. James did the same and indicated we should as well. The ritual finished, the matriarch grunted and motioned for the rest of her people to reenter the woods. Once the last of them disappeared into the foliage, James stepped out of the clearing, heading back toward the car. As I neared the edge of the clearing, I turned to find Leslie still watching the smoking pile of dirt. The look on her face spoke of a rage capable of burning down whole nations.

"Leslie?" I asked as gently as possible.

She blinked back into the present and walked out of the clearing without comment. I followed, steeling my mind against the chaos and darkness still ahead of us.

Okanogan Funeral Home

The drive back to town was silent except for when I asked James to drop us off at the sheriff's office. After we got out of the car, James offered me a slow nod and weak smile. He didn't foresee a happy ending to all this any more than I did. When the death of an innocent starts a conflict, a happy ending is all but impossible.

We found the sheriff poring over a pile of documents when we entered. He glanced up long enough to wave us over before returning to his papers.

"Anything interesting?"

"No. Mostly letters telling me to arrest the entire Colville Reservation or to resign, some financial reports, courtesy of Councilman Davers, on how the sabotage is affecting the surrounding towns, and a rental agreement listing the address of one Michele Johnson."

"The wolf leader?"

"Yeah."

"But you don't think it's her."

"Neither do you."

"I got a close look at the child's body up in the woods. Mind if I take a second look at the three men from the logging site?"

Praswá grabbed his hat and led the way. We walked to the funeral home as the sun set in the distance. Townspeople bustled up and down the streets, eyeing Praswá and me as we strode by. No one took notice of Leslie, or their attention slid over her when they tried. Just being with the two of us, a single young woman with the sheriff and an out-of-town detective, made her out of place enough that her cloaking spell weakened. Still, it did the job of keeping her outside the center of anyone's attention.

"The sasquatch said they'd give us one day before getting involved. They cremated the body as part of a ceremony."

"Blood and fire," Praswá noted. "I'm familiar." He stared ahead, taking in the buildings, streets, and sky all at once. "This has become personal for everyone. Can't say I blame them." Praswá chewed on his thoughts for a beat. "It'll be bad if we officially arrest any of the həłn'cicň'i? t c̓lc̓aɬ, let alone their leader. The whole tribe will protest, and the townspeople will use it as an excuse to blame the reservation for even more of their collective misfortunes."

"How familiar are you with all this mystical supernatural stuff?"

"Very. I was raised in the tribe. On my coming-of-age ceremony, I was introduced to the həłn'cicň' i? t c̓lc̓aɬ, the scx̌ʷanʕáy̓tm̓, and our mutual obligation. The tribe uses the opportunity to test us as well."

"Test you?" Leslie asked.

Praswá jumped a little having forgotten Leslie was with us. "To see if we carry the sxʷic̓c̓x i? t n̓c̓icň'.[1] The ceremony takes place on the first full moon after we hit puberty. That's when all həłn'cicň'i?

---

1. Gift of the Wolf. Pronounced: sqwistch·qh ee- t ench·EE·chen.

t čłčaɬ change for the first time. We must be careful that others who are strong enough are present to manage a new n̓cicn̓. The first transformation is traumatic, new həłn̓cicn̓ i? t čłčaɬ lash out in confusion and pain. It takes many of their brethren and sčxʷanʕáy̓tm̓ to restrain them without causing others and themselves harm."

"How is the condition passed along?" Leslie continued.

"Blood. At first, through family, but as time went on, not all children of the həłn̓cicn̓ i? t čłčaɬ were born with it and numbers dwindled. We discovered that the exchange of blood could pass the gift to those who wished to dedicate themselves to the cx̌a?x̌á? sčxʷxtwixʷ."

"They have the power to make more were-wolves?" I asked.

"Yes, but the passing of the gift has been tightly controlled for generations. If they made another, it would be hard to conceal. The new one would be just as wild on the first transformation. The həłn̓cicn̓ would need to gather together in great numbers to control their initiate."

Our conversation died as we passed through the doors of the funeral home which doubled as a morgue. Praswá led the way to the back of the building where he found the mortician arranging the three bodies on slabs.

"Hey, Leo. Give us a few minutes with the bodies; we need to look them over again."

"Sure thing, I already removed their clothes. If you need them, check the box over there."

Leslie hovered on the other side of the room and hugged herself against both the cold of the room and the reality of being so close to three dead bodies. I didn't think waving her over to help examine the corpses or the clothes would be useful, so I let her keep her distance. Leo had washed all the blood and mud away and placed the torn limbs where they belonged like one might set puzzle pieces near one another without connecting them. While the damage was extensive, the bodies didn't look as savaged as they had at the logging site. Something about clean bodies made it all seem less horrific.

"No doubt about it, the marks match those on the child."

"Doesn't get us any closer to an answer, though."

Using one of the scalpels on the table by the slab, I explored each slash one at a time, prying them open to see inside. I hoped for a broken claw or a shred of cloth. Anything that would point us in a direction.

"You never told me why you went out of your way to make sure all the parts were gathered and accounted for. I mean, of course you needed to eventually, but why the immediacy?"

Praswá didn't seem to want to answer but eventually he did. "It's gruesome, but if any of the body parts were missing, it would eliminate the scʼxʷanʕáyʼtmʼ. If some were gone, it would point to a younger werewolf, newly turned. They have a tendency to... eat their victims." Praswá didn't meet my eyes. "It's not something the tribe likes to discuss.

"I noticed you didn't say həłnʼcicňʼ. Why not?"

"həłnʼcicňʼ is more of a title. It's reserved for our people. None of the known həłnʼcicňʼ are young. Missing body parts would have pointed away from them." He had hoped for missing parts. Having found every limb implicated the həłnʼcicňʼ iʔ t cʼlcʼaɬ.

Going over the second body, something glinted out of one of the large wounds. After cutting the wound a little deeper, I used a pair of curved forceps to dislodge and withdraw a small metal medallion. I went over to the box of discarded clothes and wiped the medallion clean.

"Damn it."

Praswá peered over my shoulder and stopped cold. "Damn it."

Leslie stepped forward, her curiosity overcoming her revulsion. "What is it?"

The medallion, torn from the leather cord it had been hanging from, shined in the light of the room as I showed it to Leslie. "It belongs to the n̓tlʕánaʔ of the həłn̓cičn̓ iʔ t čl̓čaƚ, Michele Johnson."

Omak, Washington

The rental paperwork said Michele had a small place in Omak. We drove there, hoping to find her. It was above an old, out-of-business bar still used as a generic hangout for many different groups in town, but now the only things served were grumbled conversations and sullen silence. The stairs on the side of the building led up to her apartment.

"Should we have brought something to deal with her if she decides to change? *Can* she change during the day?"

Praswá peered at the distant sunset. "Once they've trained and gained control over their gift, they can change at will, day or night. Though, if night were required," he pointed at the disappearing sun, "it wouldn't matter. As for dealing with her? I doubt she'll give us much trouble. She cares for our people and knows if she fights, it will end up harming more innocents. She's angry but still a warrior and guardian to our tribe."

"I thought she and the others broke away."

"There is breaking away and there is abandoning. She will protect her people when required to do so."

Praswá knocked on the door with heavy, solid strikes. Michele opened the door wide and stepped back to let us in. Her place was sparse, but well-ordered. She kept the ever-present dust out. Every item in the room appeared to be arranged according to the strict phrase, "A place for everything, and everything in its place."

"What's this about, Praswá?" She offered us a gentle smile. Her casual air was a drastic change from the hardened leader I'd encountered on the clifftop. She was so subdued, I almost forgot she could change into a werewolf. When I tried to smile in return, her eyes hardened and flared yellow around her irises. The weight of my gun itched under that piercing glare. I couldn't deny her allure, nor could I ignore the extreme danger she presented.

Leslie stood in awe of the woman before her. Michele was strong, courageous, a leader, and powerful in a way she hoped to become with her small eldritch traveling library. I couldn't blame Leslie for remaining speechless.

Praswá held up the medallion. Michele touched her throat where it used to hang. "Where did you find it?"

"I'm not in the mood for games, Michele."

"What?"

"It was found with the three bodies at the logging site," I said. No reason to show all our cards.

Michele's features went cold. Within seconds she stopped being casual and shifted into her n'tlʕánaʔ persona. "And?"

"I'm going to need to take you in for questioning, Michele," Praswá replied.

"I heard it was wild animals."

"You know damn well it wasn't," Praswá said. The anger in his voice roiled beneath his words. "Three men are dead, Michele. The town is ready to boil over. I can't do much about the threat from the north, but this I can try and calm down."

"So, I'm the next to be sacrificed to the white men who stole our land and our homes?"

Praswá held the medallion in front of Michele's eyes. "Don't blame your sloppiness on me, Michele. I'm doing my job and trying to protect the rest of our people."

"Michele," I said, "I spoke with the sasquatch earlier today. They need to know who is responsible for the child's death. I don't think you or your people are guilty of that. I have until tomorrow to find an answer, or they will come down here. We need your help to figure this all out. Bringing you in could placate the townspeople long enough for us to stop something far worse from happening to everyone."

Michele gathered her distressed leather jacket. "You going to cuff me?"

"Do I need to?"

Michele led the way out the door.

Outside, the rest of the həłn̓cicn̓ i? t c̓lc̓aɫ stood at the base of the stairs. They glared at us as we descended. Praswá strode forward and confronted the crowd. "I need to bring Michele in. Don't make this worse."

"Worse for who, sheriff? You afraid if you stand up for your people and the cx̌a?x̌á? sc̓x̌ʷxtwixʷ, you'll lose the white man's jewelry?" The speaker poked Praswá in his badge.

"Willis, this has gone too far. If I don't bring her in, it'll cause a riot."

"Good." Eyes turned gold all around. Some həłn̓cicn̓ i? t c̓lc̓aɫ allowed fangs to protrude from their mouths. I pushed Leslie behind me and grasped my revolver for what good it would do us.

"Stop!" Michele shouted. "I will not have us fighting amongst ourselves. I will go with Praswá if it will prevent harm from coming to our people. Go and protect the tribe. Once word gets out about me, they will need your help." She focused on Willis. "Go tell Elder Chelahitsa what's happening. Tell him the cx̌aʔx̌áʔ sc̓x̌ʷxtwixʷ is in danger. sc̓x̌ʷanʕáy̓tm̓ comes."

Willis nodded and waved the rest of the həɬn̓cic̓n̓ iʔ t c̓lc̓aɬ away. As the crowd dispersed, we made our way back to the car.

Everything about this felt wrong. The həɬn̓cic̓n̓ iʔ t c̓lc̓aɬ didn't attack the sasquatch. They would never risk destroying a truce held for generations. But who else was there who could transform into a werewolf? Who gained from the chaos?

The sun disappeared beyond the horizon, and we headed south to Okanogan.

"I don't know who could have attacked the child up in Monashee," Michele said.

"What about a new wolf? I'm told new wolves lash out."

Michele glanced at Praswá before answering. "You are learning a lot in your investigations, Mr. Daniels. Yes, young n̓cic̓n̓ can be hard to control, but we haven't had any new additions recently. The attack in the mountains wasn't us."

"Then explain what attacked me."

Michele sunk into her seat. "I can't. I've been trying. We weren't at the logging site today because we were trying to figure it out." Michele smiled at Leslie in response to her open adoration. I took note. Another supernatural creature unaffected by the cloak.

"You weren't avoiding the dead bodies?" Praswá asked.

"I'll wait to answer any questions related to that after the tribe sends our attorney, thanks."

I grimaced. "Well, this leaves me in a bind. I need an answer for the sasquatch."

"It'll take them half a day to get down here if you don't head back. I would say we have until this time tomorrow before they take matters into their own hands."

"Which means?"

Michele shrugged. "Whatever they choose to do, it will begin with the logging site. They hate it as much, if not more, than we do."

"What about the other sasquatch already down here?"

"They will wait for their brethren to join them. Their only mission was to stall the logging operations. With everything going on now, they will stop assisting our efforts until their leader arrives."

"Is it possible one of your people made another werewolf without your knowledge?" Leslie asked.

"I've asked around. Once your associate informed us a child was killed, even the fear of tribal punishment wouldn't stop any of us from confessing they'd made an n̓cičn̓ without approval. Every n̓cičn̓ knows this threatens the cx̌aʔx̌áʔ sc̓x̌ʷxtwixʷ, and worse still, innocent lives. We may hate the logging operation, but we don't wish harm on the blameless."

When we arrived at the station, Probst stood out front like a statue, waiting. I heard groans from all around the cabin of the car. I didn't think the day could get any worse.

The Olesk Residence

The Rolls Royce idled along the curb opposite Probst. As Praswá escorted Michele into the building, Probst flashed his paper smile and said, "Sheriff, can I assume you've made an arrest this evening?"

"Ms. Johnson has agreed to come in for questioning. Unless you wish to represent her, it's none of your concern at this time."

Probst chuckled and turned his attention toward me. "Alas, I heard Mr. Daniels was in your company, and I have been asked to take him to Mr. Olesk. If he is no longer needed."

"I'll catch up with you later, Travis. It's best I take care of this as officially as I can."

"Tomorrow, then." I turned to Probst. "I'm sorry, but it's been a long day, and my friend and I need to get some sleep."

Probst noticed Leslie and paled. He recovered quickly and reached out his hand. "I'm sorry, miss, for my poor manners. I didn't see you there. Please, don't think me rude."

Leslie presented her best smile and shook his hand. "Not a problem. It happens more than you'd think."

I almost laughed. Probst considered the comment for only a moment before his eyes drifted away from Leslie and back onto me. "I understand, of course. This meeting won't take more than a few minutes and it's in Tonasket, where Mr. Olesk resides."

Without a ride back to the hotel, accepting the meeting seemed the best option. "Yeah, fine."

"Wonderful. After you." Probst waved us toward the car. Once in, Probst re-noticed Leslie and paled once more. He didn't seem the kind of man who missed even the smallest detail, and his inability to remember a young woman in close company was unmooring him. For the whole ride, Probst assailed Leslie with questions, forcing himself to focus on her and her alone. I sat back and watched, curious about the extent and power of the cloaking spell under a concerted effort to fight it. To the lawyer's credit, he never allowed his attention to waver and only a single droplet of sweat broke along his brow from the mental strain.

Few lights glowed in the windows of the residential homes on the outskirts of Tonasket. The dust kicked up by the car disappeared into darkness around us. The moon and stars shined bright enough to make out the struggling blades of grass scattered across the wide-open plots. Small houses of modest means stood against the barren landscape, but all wore the markings of financial struggle: weather-beaten wood, crooked shutters, and chipped paint.

The Rolls pulled into one of the large homes at the corner of Fourth and Antwine, three-and-a-half blocks southwest of the Whitestone Hotel. Probst opened the car door for Leslie, holding her in his view without wavering. "Mr. Olesk will see you in the study. Please, follow me." He broke eye contact with Leslie and led us into the house. The rooms were alight with both electricity and candles. From the drive, I didn't remember seeing many electrical lines running up and down the streets, so either they were all underground, or Olesk paid a great deal of money to get power out to him.

The site foreman, Williams, passed us as we crossed through the foyer. His limp was gone and in the dim light of the night, his many scars were barely visible. Only the missing arm remained as evidence of his vocation. He nodded to me as I walked past and marched out into the night toward the houses in the distance.

I tapped Probst on the shoulder. "Are any of you ever off the clock?"

"Those of us who are deemed essential are expected to always be on call, but we are paid well for our availability to Mr. Olesk."

Being a private detective forced me to keep strange hours, but I couldn't think of any amount of money that would have me working like these guys, playing escort and manager. Doing it for myself was one thing. Working for a taskmaster struck me as repugnant.

Olesk stood behind a massive mahogany desk. Carvings of growling and snarling beasts marked the corners. The borders displayed hand-engraved reliefs of stampeding animals in all shapes and sizes. On his walls hung the mounted heads of bears, deer, and antelope. Off to one corner stood a stuffed, snarling wolf. Maps and surveys, jungles, continents, and national topography papered every other empty space. I didn't see a single book that wasn't an accounting ledger anywhere. Probst strode over to Olesk, whispered in his ear, and retreated from the room.

"Quite the collection you have here," I said. The doors to the study clicked shut behind me to guarantee privacy.

"Hm? Oh, yes. I do enjoy hunting. There's some good places around here if you know where to look."

"You mentioned that when we first met. Any place better than the others?"

"Not especially. There's some good game up toward the Canadian border. When things calm down, I'll head back up there. For now, Probst tells me you and the sheriff arrested the leader of those saboteurs. Good job."

"Officially, she's volunteered to come in for questioning, but the evidence does appear to implicate her."

"Of course it does!" Olesk didn't bother to look up from the maps and reports he was going over. "Without their constant interference, we were able to repair all of our equipment. We even managed to do some cutting!" He finally glanced my way with an enormous smile. "I've asked Williams and some of his men to reach out around the towns and have anyone looking for work to report to the site tomorrow. I should be full steam ahead."

"Seems not even murder can halt progress."

"Exactly!" Olesk pounded on the desk. "America was built by white men's hands powered by a can-do determination and, by God, I'm going to see that nothing changes that." Olesk lifted a thick envelope and tossed it across his desk. "There's your fee for services rendered. Probst informed me you prefer cash. I trust this will be more than enough to cover your time and expenses."

A quick flick of my thumb over the edges revealed a nice array of ones, fives, tens, and even a few twenties. "Thanks. If you won't be needing anything else?"

Olesk waved his hand that same way one might shoo an errant fly.

Leslie blurted out, "How can you be so cold about the men who died? It's like you only care about your business and profit. What about all the blood that's been spilt?"

"And who is this?" Olesk asked with a bemused smirk.

"This is my assistant. Please don't mind her. We'll be on our way."

"Not at all. I'm always happy to educate the youth of our great nation. They are the future, after all." He wasn't surprised to have someone flash into his awareness. After years of ignoring those deemed unimportant, it probably happened often without the help of magic. "My young lady, when you grow older, I hope you meet a man who will protect you from the world, which is not a fair or safe place. People get hurt. They die. The beauty of our country is that no matter how many people fall to the wayside, there are always more desperate souls waiting to replace the weak. The man you one day meet will, I hope, have struggled and worked hard to become strong so he may protect you and provide you with a home and children. While the government pretends to drive our nation, the truth is we are a Darwinist Capitalism. Companies like mine, or the railroads, or the steel manufacturers are the beating hearts and veins that deliver the blood of commerce. Through our work and strength, we keep towns like this one and many others alive. It's a hard lesson to learn, but to have a strong nation, sometimes we must break the weak gears so better ones may take their place. I hope that helps you find the correct kind of man you should marry in the future. Good day."

I grasped Leslie's arm and pulled her out of the room before she dove across the desk and attempted to rip the old man apart. Probst stood by the front door waiting for us. He watched me drag Leslie along and strained to appear as if he wasn't surprised that he'd somehow forgotten her again.

"Would you like a ride back to your hotel?"

"No, thanks. It's only a few blocks and my friend here would do well to walk off her excitement from meeting Mr. Olesk."

Probst pursed his lips and gave me a confused look yet said nothing. He opened the front door and ushered us out.

We were nearing Tonasket Ave, a full block away from Olesk's home, before I released my grip on Leslie's arm. She grabbed my arm and wheeled me around to face her. Fury twisted her affable features. "I can't believe you! You took that bastard's money and let him talk about people like they're nothing."

"Bastard money spends just as well as righteous money. Bastards tend to pay better."

"I refuse to use any of that money."

"First off, *you* don't spend any money. *I* do. Second, you didn't have a problem with us using your uncle's money to get away from New York and stay alive for the last year."

"That's different."

"No, it really isn't. We're on the run and need to do whatever we can to remain free of Mandeville's attention. I'll take whatever money is handed to me and I will use it to keep you safe whether you like it or not."

"I'm almost twenty, Travis. I could just ditch you."

"Do it."

That stopped her. Her fury melted into a sudden sadness that killed me, but she needed to understand the dangers we faced and the reality of our situation. "I don't want you to go, Leslie, but you need to start being more careful. Who cares what that old bastard says? He offered us money. I took it. I never promised to help him keep Michele in jail or help prove her guilt."

"You're not leaving town?"

"No. I took a job, not just from Olesk, but from Elder Chelahitsa. I'm going to see it to the end, no matter what. But I need to know you're going to be careful if something happens to me."

"That's not going to—"

"It may, Leslie. This isn't over. While I'm positive she's innocent of what happened in Monashee, Michele may be guilty of killing the three men at the logging site."

"There's no way."

"We don't know for sure. Either way, I need to figure out who killed the child or a lot more people are going to get hurt."

"So, who could it be?"

I stared into the night as the lights of Olesk's house winked out. There was no proof, but it added up. Olesk admitted to hunting up in the Monashee Mountains. He hated the tribes and accused them of controlling or directing beasts to attack from the woods. Add the fact that the man, possibly in his late sixties, had the constitution of a twenty-five-year-old. The jump to making him the werewolf wasn't a far one.

"Michele said the sasquatch would make their first stop at the logging site. We need to talk to Chelahitsa tomorrow and update him. I'm worried this is going to end bloody no matter what we do. Hopefully, I can convince him to have his people steer clear of what's coming."

Leslie took my arm and leaned into me for support. My body was exhausted. Regardless, I held steady for her if not myself. We needed to survive one more day. I just couldn't see how.

Okanogan, Washington

Leslie woke up and found me staring out the window of our room.

"What are you doing?"

I nodded down toward the street. She wrapped a blanket around her and padded over to the window. Our friend and his horse waited outside. He peered up at us and nodded good morning.

"Get yourself together. I intended to visit Chelahitsa today. Seems he had a similar idea." I paused to consider my next words. "Bring your books."

She rushed away to get dressed and gather her small library. I wanted to reiterate all my warnings about relying on those books and spells too much, but considering how this day was going to likely end, I kept my mouth shut.

Once Leslie was ready, we met our friend outside. He'd already mounted his horse and was waiting for us to get my car going. Once again, we followed him to Okanogan where he disappeared into the ranch after escorting us to Chelahitsa's door. The ranch bustled with activity. A swarm of angry eyes scrutinized us as we approached the front door. A young woman granted us access before I could knock. She glared at me as if I had committed a heinous act of violence against her. Dark looks were not uncommon for me, so I chose to ignore them all and kept to my business with Chelahitsa.

"Thank you for coming, Detective."

"Elder Chelahitsa, it's good to see you again."

"You believe Michele is guilty of attacking the child?" It came out as an honest perplexity rather than a damning statement. The worry writhing in my gut eased. I hadn't even noticed it until it lightened. Experiencing any kind of emotion or concern about what a client thought of me while delivering news was unusual. Something about Chelahitsa demanded both respect and a need to be respected by him.

"No. The evidence points to her being involved in the attack at the logging site, but not the incident up north."

"The həłn'cičn' iʔ t č'ľcaľ came last night and rallied many of our people to protest the logging operation. After what James told me of your meeting, I worry this will end poorly."

"It was never going to end well."

Chelahitsa produced a slim envelope and placed it at the center of the table. "Thank you for your services, Detective. I only wish all this could have been avoided."

Something deep inside told me he would be insulted if I didn't accept, so I took the envelope without looking inside. "I'm not done yet, sir. I have a suspect, but there are still questions that need answering."

"Questions for me?"

"Sadly, no. If I thought you had the answers I needed, this would be a great deal easier. I would advise none of your people go to the logging site."

Resigned, Chelahitsa shook his head. "I have tried. The young are angry. In their passion, the cautious words of the elderly go unbidden."

A quick glance at Leslie earned me a glare. "Chelahitsa, can I ask a favor?"

He smiled and answered "Of course, your young friend can stay here with us until this is finished."

"Wait, what?" Leslie shouted. "I'm coming with you."

"No, you aren't. I don't see a way through this that doesn't end in violence. I don't want you around when all hell breaks loose at the site."

"I can take care of myself, Travis."

"I know you can, Leslie, but if I have any hope of getting through this alive, I need to know you are safe and nowhere near this fight. I trust Chelahitsa to keep you safe here at the ranch. Maybe he can even get their medicine doctor to help you learn more about what's in your books."

That stopped her arguing and left her stuck between a desire to learn more about how to use the information she "borrowed" from Miskatonic Library and the wish to stand at my side in the heat of battle. I prayed her academic leanings got the better of her for once.

"Fine, but you better come back. Don't die out there."

"I'll do what I can." I smiled and gave her a quick hug before rushing out and driving over to the sheriff's office.

I found Praswá arming up. Word of the protest must have already gotten to him. He saw me enter and waved a silent greeting.

"I need to talk to Michele."

"If you want, but she didn't say anything useful last night."

"I have a different avenue of questions to pursue. We may even need her help to get through this day with as little bloodshed as possible."

The keys for the cells in back sailed through the air and clattered into my hand. "I'll be right behind you." Three more of his deputies from the surrounding small towns came through the front door. "I need to get these men ready for what's coming." He directed them to the small armory.

I lowered my voice, "You going to tell them the truth?"

"Hell, no. I want them ready, not pissing themselves or laughing at me."

I made for the back of the station as Praswá briefed the deputies on the probable protest and the response he expected from the loggers.

Michele lay on the small cot in her cell but sat up when I approached. "I don't know what to tell you about the child—"

"I believe you."

"So why are you here?"

"Your people rallied many from the tribes to protest the logging now it's up and running again."

"Good. We need to fight back against what they're doing."

"I'm not going to argue the politics of it. I honestly don't care. But I don't want to see a lot of innocent people get hurt, which will happen if you don't help us cool things down."

"I'm sorry, but maybe that has to happen for people to start taking us seriously."

"They'll just use the violence as an excuse to pass more laws against you and restrict your freedoms even more."

"They've been doing that with and without their excuses. No one cares, and my people suffer."

"And what do you think will happen when an army of sasquatch flood out of the woods and slaughter everyone in sight? What happens when your secrets are revealed to the world? You seem to think this can't get worse, but it will."

Praswá entered. The sound of deputies loading weapons drifted back to us in a staccato of clicks and clacks. "He's right, Michele. We need to stop this."

"How?"

"First, I need to know if it's possible for you to transmit your abilities in any way other than blood? Would a scratch or bite do it?"

"No. Only sharing blood," Michele stated.

"And you never shared blood with anyone outside of the tribe?"

Michele pounced forward. "I would never! None of us would! That would be sacrilege."

Praswá burst out laughing. "She's not wrong. The həłn'cicň' i? t c'lc'aľ don't mix well with white folks. No offense." I waved it off. "Less than a week ago, I had to pull one of her younger recruits off the logging foreman for asking to buy a car for some string and beads."

"Williams mentioned that. Is that where the limp came from? I figured it was another accident on the work site."

"Yeah, kid almost killed the guy."

"Was there blood? Did the kid bust open his knuckles during the fight?" I asked.

Praswá squinted trying to understand my line of thinking.

I turned to Michele. "How much blood is necessary to change someone?"

"Not much."

Praswá's face went slack with shock as what I suggested became clear.

"But the blood sharing requires a sacred ceremony. It can't just be shared in a common fist fight," Praswá said, rationalizing how my logic stood outside the irrational world we found ourselves in.

Michele reached through the bars and touched his shoulder. "That's just a custom, Praswá. I used a small amount of my own blood to cure my cousin two seasons back when he fell ill from a wasting sickness and struggled under the weight of a relentless fever. He will turn when it is time. There is no doubt. This sort of thing has been done before. We just don't talk about it."

I fumbled with the keys, searching for the one to get Michele out of her cell. "Is there a way to hurt a werewolf? I know my gun didn't do anything."

"Yes. There is a plant commonly known as wolf's bane. It can be distilled into an oil that is lethal if fired into the heart with a treated arrow. Anywhere else will weaken but not kill."

"Leslie found much the same information in her books. Where can we get some?"

"It's extremely rare around here and the oil takes time to prepare."

"Great."

Praswá ripped the keys from my hands and proceeded to unlock the door for Michele. She exited and looked me in the eyes. Her intense focus made me stop breathing. Whatever she searched for within me, she must have found. "I have a quiver of treated arrows hidden in my apartment. We can stop there on the way. If the foreman is a n'cičn', it is my duty to stop him."

Worlds Collide

We raced to Omak to retrieve Michele's quiver and bow. The shuttered bar was cold and empty. Her compatriots and out-of-work townspeople were occupied at the logging site. I still wasn't sure about Olesk, but if it all started with Williams, he must have turned others. The werewolf I saw in the woods had two arms and Williams only had the one. However, there was the howl in the distance that preceded the monster's retreat. All I had were suppositions and hints at a larger picture. My attention snapped back to the present when Michele leapt from the car and dashed up the stairs to her apartment. As Praswá and I waited for her return, more worries and anxieties washed over me.

"You'll keep an eye on Leslie for me if I don't make it back?"

"Shut it, Daniels. We're both walking away from this mess."

"I don't believe in fairy tales. I probably should after all I've lived through recently, but it's all been nightmares and death."

"For the girl as well?"

"Maybe worse for her."

Praswá tightened his grip on the steering wheel of the car. "I'll see to her safety."

"Thanks. Just keep her out of sight. She's with Chelahitsa for now and he knows how to keep her hidden. The person looking for her is powerful and still thinks she's dead. He has to keep thinking that. But if he ever comes looking, you need to make sure there is no evidence of her ever being here."

"Shouldn't be too difficult. I'll have Chelahitsa introduce us. Strange how I've yet to meet her this whole time."

A laugh burst out of my throat, past all the worry and dread.

"What's so funny?"

"She was with us yesterday."

"No, she wasn't."

"She was." I kept laughing. "Don't worry about it. She cast a spell on herself that makes people not notice her or forget her when they do. Chelahitsa's medicine doctor strengthened it as well."

"Seriously?"

Michele returned with the bow and quiver hanging on her right shoulder to find Praswá confused and grumbling about magic while I wiped tears from my eyes, struggling to stifle my amusement. She stared at us both as if we'd lost our minds, worried she may have to deal with that as well.

"Don't ask," Praswá advised. He waved her into the car. "Let's go."

We raced down black asphalt and over dirt trails to arrive at the work site in a billowing cloud of dust. A legion of men and women, young and old, from the Confederate Tribes of the Colville Reservation stood facing grumbling workers wielding pipes, wrenches, picks, and axes. The Colville members stood unarmed, but resolute. At the front of the protesters were Michele's həłn̓cičn̓ i? t člčaľ, spread out to form a layer of protection for the collected tribes.

As Praswá maneuvered around the crowd to stand between the two sides, Michele took her place with her people, whispering to them what we suspected.

"I need everyone who does not work for Radiant Futures to disperse," Praswá announced.

Olesk stomped forward. "Disperse? I want all these people arrested for trespassing. What is she even doing here? Isn't she guilty of murdering my employees?"

"Mr. Olesk, that is still under investigation, but she volunteered to help me diffuse this situation. No one here wants to see this turn violent."

As the two men argued, I scanned the faces of the workers, looking for Williams. He didn't appear to be a part of the crowd facing off with the protesters. I caught movement out of the corner of my eye. On top of the cliff, I found Williams and four others standing at the edge, peering down. The five of them watched the drama unfold, replacing the həłn'cičn'iʔ t člcaľ as witnesses or, worse, harbingers of what came next.

Michele's attention was focused on her people while Praswá's was on the enraged Olesk.

Williams' four friends leapt off the cliff as if they were diving into a body of water. They disappeared behind a curtain of pine trees. Breathless with shock, I returned my attention to Williams at the top of the cliff. Two golden eyes pierced the distance right into me. His body began to swell as he stepped off the cliff and fell out of sight.

"Michele!" She spun around, concerned by the panicked undertone I couldn't hide. "They're coming. Five of them."

Her features relaxed into that of a seasoned warrior ready for battle. She began giving orders to her fellow protectors. Half the group stepped forward and scanned the tree line, waiting for the danger to reveal itself. The others ushered the protestors back to get them as far from the coming battle as possible.

The mysterious man on his horse galloped into view along the road. A smaller figure was riding with him. I refused to believe my first instinct, but when the horse came to a halt and turned, Leslie swung off the saddle and onto the ground. Michele gasped at the sight of the man and cast her eyes to the ground in deference.

Before I could ask anything, Leslie was at my side. "He said you sent word and needed me here?"

"What?" I glared at the man who returned my sudden rage with a hideous, predatory smile. For a brief second, his eyes flashed yellow. The grin vanished. His features returned to the placidity I'd grown accustomed to. With a snap of the reins, the horse and its rider were galloping away. Dark laughter, the kind I'd last heard in Arkham, echoed in the still-recovering parts of my mind.

"Help get these people somewhere safe."

Leslie nodded, directing everyone away.

I jogged over to Praswá and Olesk.

"If you don't tell these men to disperse, sir, I will arrest you for inciting to riot. These are your employees, and I will hold you responsible if this escalates!"

"Don't you threaten me, you savage," Olesk screamed. "I'll make sure the town council learns about how you brought a convicted killer—"

"She's barely a suspect."

"I don't care! They'll sooner believe me over someone like you. A *man* who won office on a technicality."

"Enough. Until that day comes, you will do as I say."

"Or what? You can't arrest everyone here. They'll protect me if you try to take me away."

"Sorry to interrupt, but Williams and four of his friends are coming."

"Williams?" Olesk asked. "He ran away as soon as that mob appeared. Had I known he was such a coward, I would never have kept him on after he lost his arm."

"Give it a rest, Olesk," I demanded. "I know you sent Williams or one of his friends into Monashee to start a war. You don't care who gets hurt as long as you make money."

"I will not—"

The resonant sound of wolves cut through the chaotic buzz of the voices raised in anger. Silence swept over everyone present.

When the four were-wolves crashed out of the woods, everyone choked on their communal disbelief. Inoculated against such sights, Praswá, the həłn'cicň' iʔ t c̓lc̓aɬ, and I all sprang into action. Praswá grabbed Olesk and hauled him forward to call off the were-wolves. The old man ripped himself loose from the sheriff's grasp and scuttled backward, jabbering in terror.

"The natives have summoned demons! They mean to wipe us all out!"

Half the loggers turned to face the protestors, ready to attack, but the grim stares and yellow eyes of the həłn'cicň' iʔ t c̓lc̓aɬ guarding their people gave them pause. The loggers facing the were-wolves stumbled, but to their credit, recovered their wits quickly and raised their weapons against the new, otherworldly foe.

Praswá stared after Olesk's retreating form before saying, "Guess we were wrong. He doesn't know about Williams."

"So it seems. We need to get the loggers clear."

A new set of howls from behind us sent a chill down my back and into my groin. Dark blurs of hair-covered creatures flashed around us and over the loggers. The sight brought the four were-wolves to a halt, but they roared and charged to meet their counterparts. The two sides slammed into each other, making it impossible to know who was who. As the monsters bit and clawed and slashed at one another, a fifth wolf, two-times larger than the rest and missing one arm, stalked out of the woods like death itself.

Williams, in his wolf form, leapt the distance in a single bound and slammed down like a boulder in the middle of the battle. He swiped with his single arm and swatted away the həłn'cičn' iʔ t člčaľ. Both sides seemed able to know friend from foe with ease. He waved his pack forward and charged the line of loggers. They smashed through the line of men, stampeding their once co-workers to the ground, ripping and tearing anyone in their way. I pulled as many as I could behind me and pushed them toward the gathered protesters who were being guarded by the remaining həłn'cičn' iʔ t člčaľ.

Michele directed those same protectors to enter the battle. They shifted in the blink of an eye and charged forward. The loggers, who had intended to attack the protestors, soon joined them, terrified by the massacre around them. They only knew that some of the monsters were there to protect the protestors.

Michele unslung her bow, took aim, and fired the first arrow. It cut through the air with a whisper and caught one of the four were-wolves in the chest. The beast roared in pain before crumbling to the ground and reverting into his human form. The men nearest the fighting, confused and driven mad by the impossible events unraveling all around them, ran in whichever direction they found available and free of monsters. Praswá bellowed into the din of battle, directing anyone who would listen to the relative safety of the collective group. A second wave of həɬn̓cicn̓ iʔ t c̓lc̓aʟ̓ slipped through the scattered loggers, careful not to harm any of them. Some of the workers attacked their rescuers as they ran past, but the həɬn̓cicn̓ iʔ t c̓lc̓aʟ̓ ignored the meager attempts to harm them. They intercepted the were-wolves raging through the innocent crowd. It bought Praswá time to reroute those he could. He followed the workers in their retreat, doing his best to predict where the battle would spread and avoiding it.

Michele stepped forward and took aim once again. She fired an arrow, but this one was slapped out of the air by Williams. The wolf's bane oil on the tip must have gotten on his hand. He recoiled with a snarl after deflecting the arrow. Williams roared and launched at us with lightning speed. Before I could bring my gun up to fire, Michele had changed and met Williams in midair. They crashed to the ground, clawing and biting at each other. Michele, the biggest wolf of her group, was still far smaller than Williams.

A scream from the mob tore me away from the battle. One of the were-wolves dove for the crowd. Leslie stood her ground, as the monster closed in. The scream in my throat wouldn't come out. Failure to protect her seared through my heart. Praswá lurched to try and shield her. Time slowed and his effort appeared halted as if the air itself had turned gelatinous. He wasn't going to make it.

Just as the werewolf closed in, a shield of darkness flared into existence. The werewolf bounced off the barrier. Smoke rose from his singed fur in curling, black wisps. A hitched sob of relief wracked my body.

The werewolf scratched at the ground to get away from the shield as it sucked the life from the earth to power itself. The magic was powerful, and the cost was high.

The bow and quiver were five feet away from me. I took it up, hoisted the quiver onto my shoulder, removed an arrow, and took aim. The released arrow flew forward then dropped to the ground at Michele and William's feet. Their fighting crushed it. I tried a second time, pulling the string back as far as I could. The arrow went farther but bounced off Michele's lower back with almost no force. She flashed infuriated, golden eyes my way before Williams reclaimed her attention by snapping at her throat.

"Screw this." I tossed the bow aside and withdrew another arrow. As the two leaders struggled against each other, I inched around the perimeter of the battle, gun in one hand and an arrow in the other. My only hope was to find an opening and slam the poisoned tip into Williams' broad chest. The gun wouldn't do any real good, but it may provide me with the chance to distract him.

The earth shook with the massive creatures' attempts to kill each other. Standing next to them sent vibrations rippling through me. They twisted, rolled, and crashed all around. One mistimed move and I would be crushed underneath. Williams pounced high and Michele managed to get under his bulk and use the momentum to flip him over onto his back. Using the moment, I stepped up and blasted Williams in the face, point blank. His high-pitched howl was deafening. Though no real damage was done, he still covered his face out of pure instinct. I dove forward and slammed the arrow down into Williams' chest.

He cried and lashed out, slapping me away with the force of a steam train. I tumbled through the air and landed well away from the fight. My body felt numb.

Williams clawed at the arrow, breaking the shaft, but the poisoned arrowhead remained dug in. Michele raised two clawed fists and brought them down on the wound. The agonized wail he emitted cut through the din of battle. Williams clawed at the ground, trying to drag himself to safety. Michele lifted a long metal bar and a large stone. She stabbed the bar into Williams's wound and hammered the arrowhead deeper with both steel and stone. Each strike elicited primal screams and ended with a weak whimper as the arrowhead pierced his heart. The rod tore the rest of the way through Williams's torso and into the ground, pinning him down in his death throes. The three remaining were-wolves and həłn'cičn' iʔ t člčaľ stopped mid-battle to learn what could have elicited such a sound. Michele shrunk down into her human form, gasping for breath. The closest werewolf snarled, but a golden glare from Michele gave the monster pause. At the sight of Williams's body shrinking back down to his human form, now pinioned to the ground, the remaining wounded were-wolves broke away and scurried for the northern tree line. The həłn'cičn' iʔ t člčaľ, those who could make chase, started after them, but a curt command from Michele held them back.

As the were-wolves escaped into the thick forest, a brief quiet fell over the area. Leslie allowed her shield to lower and collapsed to the ground. Praswá, loggers, and tribespeople came to her assistance. A low rumble rolled out of the northern forest. The həłn̓cicň̓ i? t čl̓čal̓ turned away, satisfied the situation was about to be dealt with, and shrunk down to rejoin the survivors. They didn't look back when yips, screams, and roars of vengeance echoed through the air. The world dimmed as I relaxed into unconsciousness.

Paying the Cost

"Travis! Get up!"

A cold ache pulsed through me until I could feel my body again, a slimy, putrid energy seeping into the depths of my soul. My spine was on fire like it had been shattered and was now being hammered back together with a general disregard for comfort. When I heaved open my eyelids, all one hundred pounds of them, I found Leslie crouched beside me. Her hands, laid on my chest, glowed with a dark purple light.

Adrenaline and fear gave me enough energy to slap her hands away and end her magical ministrations.

"Travis! Why—"

Barely above a whisper, I said, "Look down."

The drained, brittle grass being sacrificed to power the healing stabbed into my back. Leslie didn't need to look down. "I know. I figured out why the spell in the woods hurt me. I have to borrow the power from somewhere or it comes straight from me. I needed to save them." Her voice cracked now that the battle was over. "To save you."

I patted the air to assure her everything was fine. We could discuss it later. Right then, I just wanted to lie there and listen to the wind.

"You saw what they did! They summoned monsters to kill us!" Olesk screamed at anyone who would listen.

I groaned before making the attempt to sit up. Leslie helped me find my footing. Michele and her people were scavenging clothes to cover themselves while the survivors from both sides worked together to aid those injured during the attack. No one bothered to pay Olesk much attention. A collective shock hovered over the crowd like a fog. Olesk screamed in Praswá's face, but the sheriff just leaned against one of the large machines, content to have survived the battle.

Leslie helped me limp over to the sheriff as Michele and her warriors, draped under sheets to cover their nakedness, returned to help the wounded, from both sides, as best they could. Those who could, offered shawls, coats, and blankets to the həłn'cič̓n'iʔ t c̓lc̓aⱡ. The conflicting sides, protestors and loggers, came together as a community in the shadow of tragedy.

"Aren't you going to do something?" Olesk screamed. "Those... *creatures*... could turn at any second and destroy the last of my equipment! I demand they be held responsible for the damage done here today!"

"Those *people* just saved our lives," I interjected. "It was your man, Williams, and his friends who started the killing."

"Nonsense! Williams was a paragon of Radiant Futures! I'm sure they infected him somehow, turned him into that beast. He didn't know what he was doing!"

Both Praswá and I scoffed at Olesk's sudden change of heart about his employee.

"Look at them!" Leslie pointed her free hand at the mingled crowd. "The people you're blaming for this are helping your employees! They saved our lives and are making sure no one else dies because of your hate. All you can think about is money. These people are nothing more than cogs in a machine to you."

"Young lady, we are all cogs in the machine of progress." He dismissed the wounded with a wave of his hand. "Some cogs, my dear, are more easily replaced than others."

Leslie tensed, ready to surge forward and throttle the heartless businessman, but my instability reminded her how dependent I was on her at that moment. She eased back and pulled me along toward the sheriff's car. "Sheriff, if you could give us a ride back to our hotel, Travis needs rest after saving this man's life."

"Of course, as soon as I finish my business here." Praswá approached the crowd and called out. "Time to go, Michele."

She finished tying off a bandage around a logger's arm before passing through the crowd. Some stood to shield her, but she eased them aside with a faint smile.

"What are you doing? She saved us," Leslie cried out. Many rumbled their agreement.

Praswá stood firm before them all. "She's still a suspect in a murder investigation. As such, I need to bring her in."

"I understand, Praswá. I will go with you," Michele said to relax those present and avoid another incident.

The four of us made our way to the car while Olesk fumed behind us, stalking through the destruction of his logging operation. He walked past the dead bodies and appendages, ignoring them as nothing more than dross, fretting over dented and overturned machines. We all slumped into our seats after we closed the doors. The enclosed calm washed away the remains of adrenaline still in our systems.

Leslie leaned forward and poked Praswá in the shoulder. He jumped and cursed to find Leslie there. "I hate that spell." Leslie shot me a look but left it alone for now. "Why are you still bringing Michele in? Williams and his pack were the were-wolves terrorizing the sasquatch and maybe stealing cattle, so why not the three murders? They were probably trying to create tension and cause the towns to turn on the tribes."

Praswá withdrew the talisman we'd dug out of the logger's body and let it hang in the air. Michele leaned forward and covered her face. Tears seeped through her fingers. She took a deep breath and confessed. "I was so angry. Angry at all the white people taking our lands. Angry at the elders for their go-along-to-get-along attitudes. Angry at our inability to stop Olesk and people like him from raping our sacred lands. I didn't mean to kill those three men. I just wanted to wreck the equipment, but one of them attacked me. Tried to hack at me with an axe. I lost control and fought back. I killed them before my pack got me under control. We're blessed with the change, but the cost is we must always exercise a stone-like control to keep our more aggressive urges in check."

Leslie deflated as her hero in this story confessed to a tragic moment of weakness. The talisman disappeared into Praswá's pocket before we left. The drive back was quiet. We were all too tired to speak. Leslie had a faraway, lost look to her. I reached out my hand and took hers. She glanced down, then at me. "We'll need to leave tomorrow," I said. "Word of the deaths and the fight will spread.

We can't be here when reporters, or anyone else for that matter, show up." She opened her mouth to argue but didn't. She gave me one curt nod and turned back to stare at the countryside.

Once Praswá dropped us off at the hotel and Leslie helped me up the stairs to our room, I laid back and asked the question that had been burning since she showed up at the work site.

"Why did you come? I told you to stay with Elder Chelahitsa."

"The man with the horse said you needed me. Chelahitsa tried to argue, but the man insisted. It was weird. I thought Chelahitsa was in charge, but after a quick, one-sided argument, I wasn't sure anymore."

The reaction Michele had on seeing the man confirmed he was more than they had thought, but for now, I needed to sleep.

Consequences and Chaos

A loud explosion shook me from sleep. I twisted left and right, searching for an attacker, a fire, a gun, anything that would have caused that sort of sound. The room remained dark. Nothing moved within. I took a breath, then stopped when I noticed Leslie's bed empty and many of her books sprawled over it. I lurched out of bed, groaning under the strain of tight muscles. I cursed whoever had snuck in while I was asleep and injected a thin layer of acid under my skin.

Still wearing my clothes and shoes from the day before, feet aching, I made for the door. A flicker of light outside the window caught my attention. In the empty lot across the street, a small fire danced in the darkness. Under the faint glow, I saw a body crumpled beside it.

Soreness and pain be damned, I raced down the hall. Heads poked out of doors, asking about the loud noise that rattled the building. I didn't have time to waste. What would I even say?

Outside, the street was clear. I rushed to Leslie's side. She lay there, curled up, like she was camping under the stars. Lines carved into the dirt formed complex geometric patterns. At the points where the lines converged, small piles of glowing ash smoldered.

Fading into the distance, the heavy clopping of hooves filled the cold morning air.

I ran around the design, kicking over piles and scrubbing lines out of the dirt. Confident no one who didn't know what to look for wouldn't start asking the wrong questions, I scooped Leslie up and carried her back inside before anyone else came to investigate. I laid her in bed, checked her pulse, and packed our things as fast as possible.

By the time the sun came up, I was showered, shaved, and changed. Our gear was packed in the car and her books secreted into the too-small bag she'd enchanted. Leslie woke up, startled to be back in the room, and found all our belongings gone. "What?"

"I should be asking you that. Look out the window."

She rolled out of bed and approached the window with caution. Shock evinced sharp breath and sent her back a step before she turned away and covered her face. The land across the street was gray and dead. All life had been drained from the earth as far as our eyes could see. Even the wood and paint on the buildings within the blast zone had aged and rotted overnight.

"What did you do?" I demanded.

"It wasn't right that Olesk didn't pay for what he caused. I just wanted him to pay."

"Didn't you hear Michele yesterday? Her anger cost three men their lives. What will yours cost?"

"I didn't kill anyone!"

"You may have killed this whole town, Leslie!"

She fell back under the heat of my frustration. "This town depends on the logging industry. Without the work, these people have no money. Without money, how will they live? You heard what the railroad representative told the councilman. They can't afford to ship supplies without the lumber shipping out. Right or wrong, good or evil, Olesk is just a symptom of the times. People like him keep towns like this alive."

"He should just be ignored? Just be accepted?"

"No." I took a breath and tried to calm myself. "But it takes time to create change. People like Olesk overreach. They take too many risks and eventually fail. Honestly, after everyone saw how little he cared about them after the attack, I doubt anyone will go work for him, no matter how desperate they are. But what do I know? Greed is a powerful sin in all our hearts. I doubt hurting him will stop the logging or the abuse. Someone else will just slide in and continue the 'work of progress'."

"What do we do now?"

"We get moving before word spreads. Come on."

Downstairs, I tossed the room key to the man at the front desk and waved goodbye. We emerged from the hotel to find a truck double-parked beside my car and Chelahitsa sitting on the bench outside.

"Good morning, sir," I said. "I'm surprised you came out yourself and didn't send your man to meet us. He never offered his name, nor did he seem inclined to."

Chelahitsa chuckled. "I wouldn't call him 'my man', and he has left us. His work is done, and he is satisfied with his payment." At the last part, he indicated the empty, grey field across from us.

"Why would he want that?"

Chelahitsa shrugged. "Who can say what the spirits want. Our warriors asked for strength and were gifted extraordinary abilities but cursed with an unquenchable rage. My tribe is indebted to the wolf for all he's done, but he remains a predator all the same." He turned to lock eyes with Leslie. "Power always comes with a price."

The elder stood and shuffled to his truck. The passenger side door opened for him. I could see James behind the driver's seat. Chelahitsa got in, closed the door, and waved goodbye.

The truck disappeared behind a cloud of dust. "Come on. Let's get moving."

On the way out of town, we passed the local bank. I remembered the cheque Probst gave me and pulled over. "Stay here. I shouldn't be too long."

I entered the bank and found the place chaotic with activity. People were making cash withdrawals at a fevered rate. Word of the destruction at the logging site must have spread and people were preparing for what came next. I waited in line until those in front of me finished their business. The harried teller raised her eyebrows when I stepped up and handed over the cheque. "I'd like to cash this, if you don't mind."

She smiled and looked it over. She raised her finger for me to wait and walked off. She spoke with the branch manager who shook his head before trotting to the end of the line of tellers working to fulfill people's withdrawal requests.

The teller returned and said, "I'm sorry, Mr. Daniels. Mr. Olesk asked we cancel this cheque and not to honor it if it came in."

I chuckled. "Figures. Thanks, anyway."

She caught my sleeve. "Wait. I just wanted to say, we all appreciate what you and the... others did at the logging site. Most of the girls here had husbands who came home because of you and—" She wiped a tear from the corner of her eye. "—we just wanted to say thank you and that we've all suggested to our husbands they not return to work for him. Better to move and find work elsewhere than risk their lives for that monster."

I patted her hand. "It's ok. I just did the job I was hired for. I'm happy your husbands came home to you."

A small envelope was placed at her elbow which she slid forward after stuffing a few bills into it herself. "Take this."

"No, I couldn't."

"Mr. Olesk may not see fit to pay you for your services, but we do. Please."

The envelope scraped across the counter like a whisper as she pushed it toward me. The bank had fallen silent. All the tellers stopped working and watched me. Even the manager stared, ignoring the lack of work being done. Everyone present offered a smile and a silent thank you. With the envelope in hand, I tipped it against my temple and returned those glorious smiles. As I left the bank, I could hear the rustle of paper and the sound of desperation, but nothing to indicate a defeated community.

Coda

The Misters

Praswá was sitting at his desk, flipping through the newspaper, when two men dressed in dark green suits walked in. He gave them a quick assessment before going back to his reading.

A deputy ran up to greet them. "What can we do for you?"

"We wish to speak with your sheriff."

"About?"

They answered with blank stares and stony silence.

The deputy squirmed for a few seconds before backing away and running like he was being chased to Praswá's desk. "They want to speak with you, sir."

Praswá folded the paper and stood. "What can I do for you?"

They inspected Praswá before the man on the right smiled as if for the first time in his life. "We're looking for a man and young woman. We suspect they were here about a week ago? During the incident with Radiant Futures?"

"The machine accident, you mean? It was the company's fault for using substandard equipment. The new outfit seems to run a tighter ship and is even replanting the trees they cut down. Good people, so far."

"As you say," said the smiling man. "But what of the man and young woman?"

"You'll have to be more specific."

"The man is a detective, brown eyes, brown hair, older; and the girl is blonde, blue eyed, about nineteen. They would have been here last Friday, possibly passing through."

Praswá peered at the ceiling before shaking his head. "Sorry, doesn't ring a bell. But that was a crazy week. Vandalism, cattle theft, and protests. They in trouble?"

"Not at all. The young woman's family is gone, and her uncle wishes to offer his support."

"Well, good luck to you." He returned to his paper. "I think we'll all need it after last week. All the papers are calling it Black Thursday. Ominous."

Both men stood for a beat before turning and leaving. Praswá watched them go and offered a small prayer to the spirits of his people that Daniels and the girl—what was her name?—were ok. It seemed like the whole country was crumbling into dust.

ACKNOWLEDGEMENTS

While writers start a project all by their lonesome, huddled in front of a pad of paper or under the glow of a computer monitor, we inevitably come across aspects of our work where others are necessary. I'd like to take this time to thank them.

I'd like to thank Dr. Michele K. Johnson for all her assistance with translating and correcting my use of Nsyilxcn throughout the narrative of the book. Also, she was kind enough to record all the words and phrases I used in the book to help with recording the audiobook. She is doing wonderful work trying to save one of many endangered languages of indigenous peoples. Please take the time to check out her organization, The Language House, for more information: thelanguagehouse.ca.

Members of the Okanogan County Historical Society patiently and quickly provided me with maps, newspaper clippings, reference photos from 1929, and advertisements from the period to assist me in getting as many details correct as possible. Some things, like the Sheriff, were changed for narrative purposes, but streets, directions, and landmarks are as accurate as I could make them. Any errors are mine alone for not asking the right questions.

Christopher Parkins of the Salish School of Spokane is another educator fighting to keep several indigenous languages alive today. His website has a wealth of resources for those interested in the work they are doing. The Nsyilxcn Pronunciation Guide provided in the book is courtesy of the Salish School of Spokane's website: interiorsalish.com.

To my beta readers—Heather Straub, Erica Summers, and Scott Fowler—you all made wonderful suggestions that I hope you see reflected in the final draft. Every author needs fresh eyes once in a while and I was lucky enough to have three sets before sending it off to Crystal Lake, who provided several more.

Finally, a huge thank you needs to go out to the team at Crystal Lake. Thank you Joe Mynhardt, Jaco Nieuwoudt, Jamie Powell, Charlene Du Toit, Naching T. Kassa, Anita Stewart, Joanna Halerz, and Jacque Day. This book, this series, would not be out for everyone to read without your tireless work.

And as always, thank you to my wife, Stephanie, and our two kids for being patient and supportive of my writing dreams. It's not always easy, but you all help to make it work.

GLOSSARY

sc̓xʷanʕáy̓tm̓ (schwän·ĀY·tem): *Hairy Man*

N̓səʔxcĭn̓ (en·selhk·CHEEN): *Nsyilxcn, a Sylix Language*

həłn̓čĭčn̓ iʔ t c̓lc̓aʕ (hesth·ench·EE·chen ee- t tsl·tsäel): *Wolves of the Forest*

n̓čĭčn̓ (ench·EE·chen): *Wolf*

xʷuy̓st iʔ xixw̓tm̓ kʔ x̌aʔkʷilx (hüoo·ye-ST ee- hee·who·tm Kl-·Klä·QUeelh): *Take the girl to the medicine doctor.*

čx̌aʔx̌áʔ sc̓xʷxtwixʷ (chä·HA- sch·hoo·TWEE·hoo): *Sacred Agreement*

n̓tlʕánaʔ (en·tl·Ä·nā): *Pack Leader*

sxʷic̓x iʔ t n̓čĭčn̓ (sqwistch·qh ee- t ench·EE·chen): *Gift of the Wolf*

Nsyilxcn Alphabet Pronunciation Guide

Compiled by Sʕamtícaʔ (Sarah) Peterson for The Paul Creek Language Association

a	as in the word f<u>a</u>ther- a	example:	anwí (you)
c	as in the word <u>ch</u>urch- c	example:	cʕas (crash)
ċ	as in the word ca<u>ts</u>- ċ	example:	ċaɬt (cold)
ə	as in the word <u>e</u>lephant- ə	example:	əcxʷuy (goes)
h	as in the word <u>h</u>appy- h	example:	hiẃt (rat)
i	as in the word s<u>ee</u>- i	example:	ixíʔ (that / then)
k	as in the word <u>k</u>ite- k	example:	kilx (hand)
ḱ	is pronounced as a hard k- ḱ	example:	ḱast (bad)
kʷ	as in the word <u>qu</u>een- kʷ	example:	kʷint (take)
ḱʷ	is pronounced as a hard kʷ- ḱʷ	example:	ḱʷckʷact (strong)
l	as in the word <u>l</u>ove- l	example:	limt (happy)
ĺ	pronounced as an abruptly stopped l- ĺ	example:	sĺaɬt (friend)
ɬ	pronounced as a slurpy l- ɬ	example:	ɬtap (bounce/jump)
ƛ̓	pronounced as a click tl out of the side of your mouth- ƛ̓	example:	ƛ̓lap (stop)
m	as in the word <u>m</u>om- m	example:	mahúyaʔ (raccoon)
ṁ	pronounced as an abruptly ended m- ṁ	example:	Stiṁ (what)
n	as in the word <u>n</u>o- n	example:	naqs (one)
ń	pronounced as an abruptly ended n- ń	example:	níńwiʔs (later)
p	as in the word <u>p</u>op- p	example:	pńkiń (when)
ṗ	pronounced as a popped p- ṗ	example:	ṗum (brown)
q	pronounced as a k deep in the back of your throat- q	example:	qáqnaʔ (grandma)
q̓	is pronounced as a hard q- q̓	example:	q̓aʔxán (shoe)
qʷ	is pronounced q with rounded lips- qʷ	example:	qʷacqn (hat)

q̓ʷ	is pronounced as a hard q with rounded lips- q̓ʷ	example:	q̓ʷmqin (antler)
r	is rolled on your tongue- r	example:	yirncút (make itself round)
s	pronounced as in the word sister- s	example:	síyaʔ (saskatoon berry)
t	as in the word top- t	example:	tum̓ (mother)
t̓	pronounced as a hard t- t̓	example:	t̓inaʔ (ear)
u	as in the word soon- u	example:	uɫ (and)
w	as in the word walk- w	example:	wikn (I saw)
ẇ	an abruptly ended w- w	example:	sẇawẇásaʔ (auntie)
x	pronounced as a soft h in the back of the throat- x	example:	xixəẇtm (girl)
x̌	pronounced as a gutteral h deep in the back of throat- x̌	example:	x̌ast (good)
xʷ	pronounced as a h with rounded lips in the back of the throat- xʷ	example:	xʷuy (go)
x̌ʷ	pronounced as a gutteral h with rounded lips in the back of the throat- x̌ʷ	example:	x̌ʷus (foam)
y	as in the word yellow- y	example:	yus (dark / purple)
ẏ	an abruptly ended y- y	example:	ćsẏaqn (head)
ʕ	pronounced like a short a deep in the back of the throat- ʕ	example:	ʕaymt (angry)
ʕ̓	pronounced as an abruptly ended ʕ- ʕ̓	example:	ʕ̓aćnt (look)
ʕʷ	pronounced as a nasally "ow" back in the throat- ʕʷ	example:	kaʕʷm (pray)
ʔ	is a breath stop in the back of the throat as in the word "uhoh"- ʔ	example:	ʔaʔúsaʔ (egg)

ABOUT THE AUTHOR

JP Behrens is the author of *Portrait of a Nuclear Family*, *We Don't Talk Anymore and Other Dark Fictions*, and the *Travis Daniels Investigations Series*. A graduate of the Yale Writers' Workshop, he spends his days writing, reading, and practicing Kung Fu. All his other time is spent with family. He looks forward to revisiting sleep one day.

For more from JP Behrens, consider joining his Patreon. A paid membership gives readers a monthly short story, a chapter a month in an ongoing thriller novel, articles, and personal essays. Sometimes, he will send out surprise gifts to his long-term supporters.

THE END?

Not if you want to dive into more of Crystal Lake Publishing's Tales from the Darkest Depths!

Check out our amazing website and online store or download our latest catalog here.

We always have great new projects and content on the website to dive into, as well as a newsletter, behind the scenes options, social media platforms, our own dark fiction shared-world series and our very own webstore. Our webstore even has categories specifically for KU books, non-fiction, anthologies, and of course more novels and novellas.

Readers...

Thank you for reading *Murder in the Monashee Mountains*. We hope you enjoyed this novel. If you have a moment, please review *Murder in the Monashee Mountains* at the store where you bought it.

Help other readers by telling them why you enjoyed this book. No need to write an in-depth discussion. Even a single sentence will be greatly appreciated. Reviews go a long way to helping a book sell, and is great for an author's career. It'll also help us to continue publishing quality books.

Thank you again for taking the time to journey with Crystal Lake Publishing.

You will find links to all our social media platforms on our Linktree page.
https://linktr.ee/CrystalLakePublishing

Follow us on Amazon:

MISSION STATEMENT

Since its founding in August 2012, Crystal Lake has quickly become one of the world's leading publishers of Dark Fiction and Horror books. In 2023, Crystal Lake officially transitioned into an entertainment company, joining several other divisions, genres, and imprints, including Torrid Waters, Sinister Smile Press, Crystal Lake Comics, Crystal Lake Games, Crystal Cove Press, Crystal Lake Kids, Memento Mori Ink, and The House of Shadows & Ink on YouTube.

While we strive to present only the highest quality fiction and entertainment, we also endeavor to support authors along their writing journey. We offer our time and experience in non-fiction projects, as well as author mentoring and services, at competitive prices.

With several Bram Stoker Award wins and many other wins and nominations (including the HWA's Specialty Press Award), Crystal Lake puts integrity, honor, and respect at the forefront of our publishing operations.

We strive for each book and outreach program we spearhead to not only entertain and touch or comment on issues that affect our readers, but also to strengthen and support the Dark Fiction field and its authors.

Not only do we find and publish authors we believe are destined for greatness, but we strive to work with men and women who endeavor to be decent human beings who care more for others than themselves, while still being hard-working, driven, and passionate artists and storytellers.

Crystal Lake is and will always be a beacon of what passion and dedication, combined with overwhelming teamwork and respect, can accomplish. We endeavor to know each and every one of our readers, while building personal relationships with our authors, reviewers, bloggers, podcasters, bookstores, and libraries.

We will be as trustworthy, forthright, and transparent as any business can be, while also keeping most of the headaches away from our authors, since it's our job to solve the problems so they can stay in a creative mind. Which of course also means paying our authors.

We do not just publish books, we present to you worlds within your world, doors within your mind, from talented authors who sacrifice so much for a moment of your time.

There are some amazing small presses out there, and through collaboration and open forums we will continue to support other presses in the goal of helping authors and showing the world what quality small presses are capable of accomplishing. No one wins when a small press goes down, so we will always be there to support hardworking, legitimate presses and their authors. We don't see Crystal Lake as the best press out there, but we will always strive to be the best, strive to be the most interactive and grateful, and even blessed press around. No matter what happens over time, we will also take our mission very seriously while appreciating where we are and enjoying the journey.

What do we offer our authors that they can't do for themselves through self-publishing?

We are big supporters of self-publishing (especially hybrid publishing), if done with care, patience, and planning. However, not every author has the time or inclination to do market research, advertise, and set up book launch strategies. Although a lot of authors are successful in doing it all, strong small presses will always be there for the authors who just want to do what they do best: write.

What we offer is experience, industry knowledge, contacts and trust built up over years. And due to our strong brand and trusting fanbase, every Crystal Lake book comes with weight of respect. In time our fans begin to trust our judgment and will try a new author purely based on our support of said author.

To date we've published around 300 books, and with each launch we strive to fine-tune our approach, learn from our mistakes, and increase our reach. We continue to assure our authors that we're here for them and that we'll carry the weight of the launch and deal with third parties while they focus on their strengths—be it writing, interviews, blogs, signings, etc.

We also offer several mentoring packages to authors that include knowledge and skills they can use in both traditional and self-publishing endeavors. This includes Shadows & Ink Creators on our The House of Shadows & Ink YouTube channel and our Crystal Lake Academy.

We look forward to launching many new careers.

This is what we believe in. What we stand for. This will be our legacy.

Welcome to Crystal Lake Publishing—Where Stories Come Alive!